FALLEN

FALLEN

ALEXA WHITEWOLF

Fallen
A Demoni Sancti Novel

by Alexa Whitewolf
Copyright ©2020 Alexa Whitewolf

Cover design by Y. Nikolova at Ammonia Book Covers

ISBN: 978-1-989384-12-1

This is a work of fiction.

Names, characters, places, and incidents either are the product of the author's imagination or fictitiously, and any resemblance to actual persons, living or dead, business establishments, events, or locales is entirely coincidental.

10 9 8 7 6 5 4 3 2 1

QUICK AUTHOR'S NOTE

This first novel in the *Demoni Sancti* urban fantasy series takes place in the same universe as *Blazing Ashes* (also available on Kindle Unlimited!). You don't have to read *Blazing Ashes* in order to enjoy this series, but it will provide more context – plus, you get to see Dante and Daymun bickering 😊

GLOSSARY

Not as much Romanian here as in *Blazing Ashes*, but it still deserves a quick mention!

Da/nu – yes/no
Foarte bine – very well
Magie – magic
Scuze / bine – I'm sorry / good
Vârcolaci – werewolves
Vârful Moldoveanu – Moldoveanu Peak

"The more I love humanity in general, the less I love man in particular."

Fyodor Dostoevsky

Prologue

Beneath the ground, the creatures awaited, swirling and growling, their souls lost to the Darkness, to the fire awaiting them in Hell. They knew she was near, that this was her choosing time.

Every five hundred years they waited, hoping it would be their turn. Every five hundred years, a Chosen One arose, to purge the world of evil through releasing Hell's wrath upon it or cleansing it with Heaven's touch.

Sometimes, the Chosen One released them from their prison in Hell. And sometimes she didn't.

This time, the rumbling of the blazes increased, and their cries grew stronger. A crack echoed above... and then through the earth. Excitement spread through the horde.

Pieces of the ground fell apart and light shone through in their prison. They stopped their movements, staring in surprise, in amazement. The brief illumination was a promise, like dangling a bone to a dog, yet it was real.

She had chosen.

She had released them.

And now... The time for purging had arrived.

With gleeful cackles and inhuman noises, they broke through the earth, ready... hungry... *starving for souls...*

Dante stood hidden in the trees, his angel wings bristling with anticipation. For nearly twenty-five years, he and another had coached a unique shifter—a Flama, whose purpose on Earth was to either cleanse humanity through opening Heaven's gate or purging it through Hell's gate. One of their kind was born every five hundred years, and this one… This one was unlike all others.

Katya's quest was filled with treacherous decisions and unwelcome—and welcome—surprises. None more than the fact she had found love amid the entire mess. She'd answered three trials, each worse than the last, to show her both the Light and Dark sides of the world whose fate she was to decide.

And through it all, Dante and his companion, a demon from Hell, provided balance, coaching and guidance. His superior in Heaven had instructed him clearly to ensure she *made the right decision*.

Yet Dante hadn't wanted to influence Katya's decisions. On the contrary, he had done his best to show her the good, while still dreading what her choice would do to the land humans called home.

Now, from afar, he watched as she changed to a phoenix, her true Flama shape. In a burst of blazes, her beautiful blazing wings soaring in the air… Then she dropped back down. Transformed back to human. Took out the ritualistic knife. Cut her palm. Her gaze went to the skies, and then below…

And when she spoke, his entire world shattered. His angel wings fluttered in the air once, twice, in shock. He watched with tears in his eyes as the ground beneath him shook, and the first of the demons escaped.

Not even Heaven can save them now...

Farther away, Daymun's gaze lingered on his protégée. For twenty-five years, he had watched over her, learned everything there was to know. He had been prepared to influence her the way he was expected to—the way he had been told to. Demons never played fair, and he'd been clearly instructed by his own superiors to do whatever needed to be done to ensure this particular victory would be theirs.

And yet, when it came to it, he was unable to. Katya's strength and perseverance deserved better than to be fucked around with. She won him through her grit and persistence, her perseverance when things were bleak. She didn't have a peaceful life, and the world had not been kind to her. To top it off, the three trials she'd been forced to withstand slowly ate at her sanity.

First, with the zmeu—the dragon hidden deep within the mountains. He'd shown her the good side of humanity, everything deserving of saving. Then, with the Fae queen, Daria, lover of Darkness, who'd presented her the evil side, and so much more. That trial rocked Katya to the core, and him along with her. Her axis, her view of right and wrong was so altered, she even feared him and Dante, her celestial guardian.

And that was not the final outcome. The last trial, the one meant to cement her choice, was toyed with. Instead of a single task, Katya was forced to two. One in a realm no one should have been able to access, older than the creation of the world. And another in the earthly grounds where she nearly lost her life to a muroni—a vampire of the caves.

And still, she had survived. She had stood strong, found her mate—with a little help—and now she made her choice.

He searched the skies, looking for his counterpart, trying to see if he was still around to witness his victory. But he was not.

It surprised him. They had both promised

her to be nearby for the final choice, whatever that might be. And as he watched his proud Flama protégée from a distance, an odd stirring rose within him. She touched him, in a way no one had in all his eons of existence.

As a demon, feelings were not what he was used to. The odd warmth in his chest was even more unheard of. He rubbed at it over his shirt, trying to make it go away, but it only seemed to increase.

And when the ground shook, and the demons emerged, Daymun let out a sigh.

He should have been happy. And yet…

Chapter 1

Dante

What a shame.

Dante wiped at his eyes, telling himself it was useless to cry over what was done. And yet, while he kept himself invisible to demons, in as much as he could, his thoughts were sporadic.

Being an angel and having lost control of his charge to the point she'd chosen Darkness instead of Light, did not bode well for his return to Heaven. Dante shouldn't have cared, after all he had been given clear instructions by his archangel superior, Gabriel. The fact he didn't follow them... and allowed other events to pass...

Katya had been a mighty Flama. He had hoped she would have chosen Heaven, much like the last one... Heaven needed a win, especially as the world of humans descended farther into chaos and demons got the upper hand over influencing them.

But despite his best wishes and lackluster efforts, Katya went through her trials and chose Hell. And though Dante didn't blame his demon counterpart Daymun for her decision, the sense of failure weighed heavily on his shoulders.

The scent of the forest all around him changed. To the demons, he remained invisible, but that did not mean he had an easier time witnessing their victory. On the contrary. As he watched their misshapen forms crawl over the ground, groaning and growling their hunger, he shuddered. Millions of humans would die because of Katya's choice. Some deserved it. Some were the scum of the Earth. But what of the innocents?

Shaking his head, Dante unfurled his ivory wings and pushed off the ground. There was no stopping it, now that it been set into motion.

Time to return to Heaven's gate, and my Silver City beyond it.

It had been a while since he'd last flown the way home. Being a guardian to Katya had meant being around her twenty-four-seven, even if she could not see him. Despite the years, it still came to him easily.

Higher into the sky he flew, like Icarus heading for the sun. But unlike the mythical hero, his wings would not melt off his back. On the contrary, they were bringing him ever higher, to the gate mortals wished they knew about to achieve eternal bliss.

Heaven was, for all intents and purposes, just another realm, accessible to angels and human souls alone. The only entrance was through a portal above the clouds, always situated under the North Star. As for what allowed said entrance? For angels, it was their blood. For the souls, it was the angels who sought them out, escorting them to the gate and granting them access to their eternal rest.

As he flew, Dante breathed in the air, which grew sparser the higher he went. The wind underneath his wings increased, and he caught that sense that he was close. Soon, a vortex pulled him in, but the power of his wings was such he managed a rather swift entrance, shaking off the tingle caused when entering the portal. Like a hand caressing his feathers, it was both soothing and made him bristle, then released him on the other side.

Clouds, puffy and white, expanded as far as the eye could see. Some reflected the sun's rays, others the light of dawn. Others still glinted silver from the essence in the air. Dante lingered above them, flapping his wings.

He touched the first cloud with his bare toe, then the second, and they formed into stairs for him. With each step, he forced himself to purge his mind of what lay below, of the innocence now being wiped away. Humanity would never be the same—but that was not his problem. Angels were not to interfere in human affairs, the rule could not be clearer.

He had been given a task, and he had done it to the best of his ability. But if he didn't wipe those thoughts, he would not be able to enter his home.

After all, only the purest of mind and intent were allowed in. Which, in truth, only added to humans believing a single sin would bar their access to Heaven. As if saints truly existed.

Dante forced back a chuckle—now was not the time.

Still, he hesitated, his mind stretching over too many considerations. Humans were one, yes. The other was much closer to his heart. After twenty-five years of watching over Katya, he cared for her. More than an angel should, more than anyone of his status should. But he could not stop it, any more than he could stop the humans' pain, any more than he had been able to stop her choice.

Had she survived? Was she safe somewhere with Vasile, her mate? Or had her choice consumed her, leading her to the Ether—the resting place of all Flamas? Did it matter, when her task was done, and he wouldn't see her again? And worse, like a nagging bee, was another thought. Now that he'd been out of the Silver City, could he return home and unsee it all?

"Enough." Dante glanced around, making sure no one heard him.

It would not be uncommon for angels to linger. Their invisibility was void past the portal, and to each other's eyes, but luckily there were none in the area. He wiped a hand over his face and forced his mind into blankness.

None of it mattered. Everything was done. And there was nothing left for him to consider... except return to his eternal rest.

Finally, step by step, he reached the intricate gate. And after a moment's silence, it opened for him. A wash of icy air cast over his skin. For a moment, the ebony hue turned pale, absorbing it in—the cleansing of all things impure.

Then it was gone, and he stepped on more clouds that transformed into marble flooring, cool against his soles. Behind him, the gate closed silently. And as Dante turned to it once more, he could not help the impression of being locked inside, of his freedom of the last twenty-five years vanishing like dew in the morning.

He shook the sensation off and moved farther inside. At the top of the staircase was another marble path leading to a large garden. Not *the* garden, but a similar one the Creator had chosen for them. His angels, His warriors, His guardians.

Tufts of green grass shone starkly against the whiteness of the trees' bark. Much like the clouds, the green reflected various shades, depending on the viewpoint. As for the trees, they were as real as one could get in this realm, their leaves silver and shining. Angels used them as their own meditating abodes, much preferring them to the chambers they were given in His House.

Dante stepped through the small vine archway, his eyes catching sight of a few celestials he'd known what seemed like eons ago. Some were chattering in groups, others were perched on the trees themselves, gazing into the distance with faraway stares.

And then Ramona landed in front of him. Long, light blonde hair, beautiful brown eyes tinged with honey, as warm as the sun's rays. Her off-white wings shook once, twice, then she folded them against her back, revealing the darker gray streaks within them. Finally, she smiled and opened her arms.

"Welcome home, Dante."

And because he wanted something normal, something that reminded him this was where he belonged, he hugged her. Buried his head in the crook of her neck, picking her up and twirling her in the air. Her wings fluttered around them, in tune with her rich laugh.

Only once he dropped her back did he realize they'd attracted attention. His display was not a normal one, not in a place where everyone took care with their feelings, and ensured they were always in control.

Ramona smiled, albeit tentatively. "That was…new."

"My apologies." Dante cleared his throat. "I have missed home and been away far too long."

She said nothing, only watched him with those eyes. And he found himself unable to meet them. He'd known her for ages, they'd had more than a passing friendship. So why couldn't he? What was wrong with him, that he felt so out of sorts? Should he have waited a few days before returning? Taken more time to meditate himself into oblivion?

"It is fine," Ramona said, taking a step closer. "I have missed *you*."

A smile escaped him, then. Without taking stock of who was watching, he arched an eyebrow. "Race me?"

Her grin could have lighted a city. But Dante was already running—only, he wasn't just running for show. His emotions in shambles, he could only hope he would eventually adjust, and not have to spend eternity outrunning them.

"Are you alright?"

Dante looked up from the grass he'd been fiddling with. "Of course." Away from all prying eyes now, in a quieter corner of yet another garden, he'd found himself drawing inward once more.

"Only... You do not look it. You seem pensive, is all."

He shrugged and let himself fall onto the grass, his wings tightly hugging his back. To his right, the light of the dying sun filtered around Ramona's shape, making her seem even more ethereal than she was.

"I watched over you, you know."

Dante smiled, tugging on a stray lock flying his way. "Did you really?"

Ramona suddenly found the grass much more interesting than him. He thought it endearing. After all, she was a younger angel than himself. But way before Katya had drawn his attention and forced him to think outside the tight celestial box he'd been placed into, Ramona had already toyed with the strings of his mind, of his curiosity, and unraveled a deep thirst of knowledge.

The reminder made him smile, and he probed again. "Through all these years?"

"You think highly of yourself!" Ramona snorted. "*No,* not the full twenty-five years. Just... Every once in a while, when I could sneak a look. I saw you with that demon, with the

British accent. The other guardian."

It was Dante's turn at scoff at the reminder of his companion. "Daymun is not British. Demons have no nationalities."

Ramona tilted her head to the side. "Then, why the accent?"

"One of his first trips on Earth was in England. You could say he took a liking to it, from what he told me." Dante shrugged. "The accent stuck. He uses it in the worst way he wants, too. Using terms like *mate* and *love* as gender specific instead of how they are supposed to be—"

He stopped, realizing he'd gone on a tangent. Cleared his throat.

"You sound like you miss him," Ramona pointed out.

Unable to stop himself, Dante lifted a hand and wrapped one of her long, blonde locks around it. "I missed *you*." The confession left his lips much too easily.

Ramona's eyes widened. Dante knew such admittances weren't normal, not with him. Not when he was so put together, so held back, so... cold. Or, rather, *had* been.

His hand fell from her hair, but she caught it and moved just that bit closer. The softness of her gown caressed his naked ribs. She reached a hand out, turning his face towards her, searching his gaze. And then she drifted closer, her hair a curtain around them, and kissed him softly.

Eons ago, before he'd gotten the assignment for Katya, Dante had been involved with Ramona. Not to this extent. Never to this extent. The way his body burned now was unlike before. The way he wanted to touch her, to possess her body...

His hand reached up to cup her cheek, at the same time grabbing a handful of hair. Not harshly, just enough for control. To hold her steady. To continue kissing her. His other hand moved over her thigh, pushing past the robe covering her limbs, and sliding farther...

Ramona gasped and pulled away from him. Dante froze. She stared at him as if seeing him for the first time, her cheeks flushed and eyes dark with desire. He knew, without a doubt, that she wasn't seeing his usually collected self, either.

The Creator made humans in his image. Angels were above that, superior to the whims of regular emotions. Yet much as they were meant to be impartial, their interactions with individuals sometimes resulted in unforeseen consequences, and changes to their own way of thinking.

"Dante!" The voice came from afar, with a slight youthful tinge to it.

He jumped to his feet, unfurling his wings to give Ramona time to fix herself behind him, hiding her from anyone else's eyes. The young angel who ran towards them seemed freshly anointed. Eyes bright with hope, with questions, he stopped a few feet away.

"My apologies, but archangel Gabriel wishes to see you."

A flicker of annoyance passed through Dante. He had expected summons of some sort, but it seemed Gabriel wouldn't even give him a moment to bask in his return.

"Tell him I will be with him shortly."

The young angel cleared his throat, shifting from foot to foot. "He insisted for it to be now."

Behind him, Dante felt Ramona stand and

dropped his wings. The angel's eyes widened, noticing her, and a faint blush colored his cheeks. Celestial liaisons weren't forbidden, but they weren't encouraged, either. Yet there were perks that came with Dante's years of experience, after all.

"Go," Ramona whispered for his ears only. "We can pick this up later."

Dante hesitated. Part of him knew he could not dismiss Gabriel's summoning. As an Elder, his word was law in these parts. And given he had only just returned...

With a sigh, he nodded and turned his attention to the young angel. "Lead the way."

Dante was led towards the massive enclosure at the other end of the garden Ramona was in. His House was, from a distance, set up like an old, white Victorian mansion, with an equally white tower and painted glass windows.

Despite the outside creative architecture, the inside was only a bare, bereft home. Chambers were there for angels to use at their discretion. Though they needed little sleep, some engaged in other activities that required seclusion, and others still led more private lives. The rooms were at their disposal, though their bareness led most of them into seeking refuge elsewhere—like the trees, or gardens in Heaven.

Oddly, Gabriel wasn't in the House itself. Instead, the young angel walked past it and brought Dante all the way back to the edge of Heaven—the gate again—and left him there. He stepped down the marble steps until he reached Gabriel.

The archangel was facing outwards, his wings and dark, raven hair tinged with silver the only visible part of him.

"You called for me?"

Gabriel turned, his green eyes piercing. Collected. "Mm. Welcome home."

Kind words, if only they were said in anything other than the cool tone used. Dante frowned. The last time he'd seen Gabriel, he'd intervened to remind him to keep Katya on track. To do what he was supposed to.

"Thank you."

Silence lingered, and Gabriel seemed in no hurry to cut it.

"Was there a purpose to this?" Dante barely kept the bite out of his voice. He failed.

Gabriel's back became rigid, his wings unfurling to their maximum capacity. A show of anger—of intimidation. "I dare say, you have learned bad habits from your time on Earth."

Dante bit his tongue. It was not appropriate for him to correct an Elder.

"You should remember you are only a Guardian, and thus you report directly to one of us."

Guardians like Dante were angels assigned to a human. Warriors were the ones who would have escaped Heaven, had Katya chosen otherwise. But as far as Heaven was concerned, Elders—mainly comprised of archangels—ran the show.

"I do recall that."

"Do you?" Gabriel arched an eyebrow. "Then do your duty. Report."

Dante's wings fluttered as he shifted his weight, widening his stance. He didn't mean it to seem threatening, but judging by Gabriel's darkening expression, he had crossed yet another line.

Rebellion was not a part of him, never had been, but in that moment, Dante wanted to be every bit the rebellious human teenager. Only, he could not afford to. Bad things happened to angels who disputed the lay of the land, as the few fallen ones could attest to.

Instead, he cleared his throat and forced a level tone. "There is nothing to say. Katya made her choice, as she was meant to. And it was not Heaven."

"I can see that."

Dante glanced at the gate, unable to stop himself.

"Go on," Gabriel said. "Look and see for yourself the suffering she has wrought on Earth."

"I do not need to see."

A frown. "Why not?"

"Because my duty with her is done, and I have returned home. I cannot care for the rest, nor attempt to change it." *There. It should be enough to satisfy him that I have not gone rogue.*

Gabriel smiled. "So, you did not forget your celestial roots, then."

The itch to clench his fists was upon him, but Dante fought it off. He should have known this was what Gabriel chased. A reason to show he was not doing his duties. Something to put a black mark on his spotless record. He did not know why the archangel had it in for him, but he suspected it was tied to the fact he'd trusted no angel since Lucifer himself.

"Never," Dante said simply.

"Very well. Let us put this to pasture, then. So, after a quarter of a century guarding this Flama in a way that—for the most part—befitted one of Heaven's Guardians, you failed to ensure her focus was on the task, did a semi-decent job in defending her and watched as she made her choice. Which happened to be Hell and thus resulted in releasing demons upon Earth, correct?"

"Yes," Dante answered through gritted teeth.

"And did she survive?"

A jolt of hope ran through him. If Gabriel was asking.... Dante told himself it did not matter. It could not matter, not to him. Any display of interest would only suit Gabriel's narrative.

"I do not know."

"You did not investigate?"

"No."

Gabriel nodded. "Very well. In that case, you are cleared to return home."

"Cleared?"

"Some of us had our doubts. That you perhaps lost your way. That you may need more than just...cleansing...for your arrival home to be complete." He offered a cool smile. "Clearly, that is not the case."

He stepped closer and grabbed his shoulders, squeezing them. "Welcome home, Dante. Let us forget the past and all it holds, yes?"

He nodded, knowing in his gut there was no other answer to give. Then Gabriel left, leaving Dante to his thoughts.

So close to the gate, it would take only a few steps to see what was happening. Time was different up there. In the few hours he had been home, weeks, if not months, would have passed on Earth. How bad was the destruction? How many lives were already lost?

And most of all, *was* Katya still alive?

Dante forced himself to turn his back on the gate, knowing it was none of his business. He was a Guardian, and he had completed his duty. What became of his charge should not matter. And yet, it did.

Why was Gabriel so keen on forgetting the past? And what was the purpose of this little show of power, if not to put him in his place?

Chapter 2

Daymun

The surrounding heat was oppressive, but none of it affected Daymun. Not a bead of sweat escaped him or dirtied his newly pressed suit. As a demon of Hell, he had the privilege to enter and leave the realm as he chose.

And though he'd expected to have missed some of it, the fiery walls, ashy ground and long, dark tunnels filled with chambers left him surprisingly indifferent. Once in Hell, he'd gone straight to his quarters to change, before reemerging in the midst of a celebration.

Demons of all shapes and sizes were doing back flips and enjoying the fun. Some chose human-like appearances, others preferred a half-animal, half-human disposition, with tails, or ears, or claws. And still others kept their reptilian forms, or their worm-like displays.

Fun, for them, was in the form of massive celebrations in one of the many acoustic caves. Walls of fire surrounded them, and lesser demons or humans were tortured into providing music—and other forms of entertainment.

Dante watched one such unfortunate soul as he juggled his own feet. It seemed a demon had found it amusing to cut them off, nail him to the ground with stakes, and watch as he struggled. Since the man was already dead, his poor soul weighed with past sins and guilt, he would not be escaping his torture anytime soon.

Still, despite the many bodies, Hell seemed emptier. It shouldn't have been surprising, given a third of all their wrath was now upon Earth, decimating its population and instilling suffering and despair everywhere they skulked.

It was a common misconception that demons only ate humans. Some lived off the flesh, others lived off manipulations, and others still lived off the energies of humans. Envy, lust, depression... It took all kinds to fuel Hell.

"Back so soon, then?"

Daymun stopped walking and turned from a particularly lusty pair of demons to face the one hiding in the shadows.

"Leviathan," he greeted him coolly.

Only his head emerged from the shadows, slimy and beady. The rest of its massive, worm-like body, easily three times Daymun's size, rolled in the darkness. Mustard-colored eyes stared back, and the words came from two incisions on either side of the head.

Daymun wrinkled his nose at the scent of fish coming off him. "Would it kill you to take a bath?"

Leviathan let out a gurgling sound. "You should watch how you speak to your superiors."

"Yeah, yeah."

Daymun glanced around. He had expected a welcoming committee of some sort. After all, his protégée had just set Hell to be the new power on Earth. The lack of one was... concerning, to say the least. Had he fallen out of favor?

It was not unheard of, for demons to backstab each other. The only thing that kept everyone in line was Lucifer and his six Princes of Hell—not to mention their respective armies. Leviathan was one, and his horde of demons were known to feed off envy. Asmodeus was yet another, with lust as his currency. In the last few centuries, they had been the most active in machinations.

And while Leviathan was right—that he was his superior—Daymun was more concerned about the other absences. What of the other five that helped Lucifer rule Hell?

"Where is everyone?"

Another gurgling laugh. "Out and about. The one you seek awaits you farther in."

Daymun nodded, and though he turned his back, he made sure to keep his senses alert. Something smelled funky. And he should know. He'd been head of rebellions and machinations, what felt like eons ago. Had it really been twenty-five years since he'd last been home?

As he moved through the crowd, various demonic dialects were thrown at him in gurgles and clicking of tongues. Most of them were congratulating, others asked whether he'd consider taking them on his next assignment. He was not surprised. After all, he was known as an overachiever.

He passed through a lake of fire, then up some charred steps that glinted like black marble. Finally, he entered a large cave set up as a banquet. Torches on either side. A long table, filled with food of all types—all of it an illusion, Daymun knew.

And in the middle, some demonesses in their human form, and Asmodeus. The demon's dark skin glowed in the firelight, but his eyes did not miss the new arrival.

"Daymun, at last returned." He clapped once, twice. "Come, join me."

The sensation in his gut intensified, wondering what trap he had stepped into now. Life in Hell was never free of issues, that much he had learned the hard way. Born to one of Lucifer's right-hand soldiers, Daymun had been chosen for various assignments from his inception. But some were always envious. None more than the demon of wrath, yet another of Lucifer's Princes, and his superior during the mission with Katya.

"Asmodeus." He inclined his head, as one would to a higher-up.

But it was not enough for the demon. One dark eyebrow arched, and he lifted his index. The moment after, an unholy force pushed on Daymun's spine, forcing him to bow or risk having it broken. He gritted his teeth and did as beckoned, going on one knee and lowering his head. After long, painful moments, the pressure finally eased. He didn't have to look up to see Asmodeus' smirk.

Some demons did what they had to in order to survive. After all, many of them had been humans, eons earlier, now contorted into unsightly beings by the force of their own guilt and emotions. And then there were some who, like Asmodeus, thoroughly enjoyed what they did. Sadistic, one could say.

"My lord." Daymun swallowed the curses wanting to pass his lips. No one was around, and no one would care.

"That is better, much better. One must follow etiquette around one's superiors, no?"

Daymun bit his cheek to avoid answering, tasting the blood. Asmodeus had been first to come on Earth and remind him of his duty. Same as Dante's superiors had done for him. Which meant, whatever game was being played, was not yet done.

The demoness on Asmodeus' lap squealed as she was tossed off him, then scurried away. Daymun knew she should count herself lucky, considering what the bastard had done to others in the past.

"Tell me, *lord*, what brings up this punishment?"

"Punishment?" Asmodeus laughed, long and brittle. His chair scraped the floor as he stood. "Punishment... No, if it was a punishment, you would know it."

He was in Daymun's face the second after, a fire harsher than a torch's in his hand. "You would *feel* it."

He pushed it closer to his cheek, and Daymun's flesh sizzled as it connected. He gritted his teeth, glaring at the demon without saying anything. Asmodeus loved to inflict pain just for the sake of it, after all, he fed off it as easily as lust.

The smell of charred flesh filled the room. Asmodeus narrowed his eyes. When he saw Daymun wasn't giving in, he dropped the fire and stood again.

"You did well, influencing the Flama to choose Darkness."

Daymun kept his mouth shut. He had done nothing of the sort. Katya had chosen of her own accord, and despite the instructions he'd received from Asmodeus, he had not contributed to it as he much as he should have. He'd gotten distracted. Too much.

The side of his cheek stung and hurt as the flesh re-aligned and healed, slowly. Rankings among demons affected the degree of suffering they were able to inflict on each other. Given Asmodeus much out-ranked him, the level of pain was higher – and it would take much, much longer to heal. Despite it, Daymun remained an immobile statue.

"It is too bad you did not notify us of the way she was leaning. We could have prepared an orderly army, instead of the mass of confusion that unfurled onto Earth. But, nonetheless, it is done. And victory is ours."

Daymun chanced a look at the demon. He was back by the table, tapping the polished wood with a fake, pensive expression. A moment later, he grabbed a leg of some kind of meat, and tossed it at his feet like he would for a dog.

"Your reward is that you get to keep your head. Now get out."

Daymun swallowed his rage and stood, leaving the meat behind.

"Ho, ho, ho. The prodigal demon returns."

Daymun turned to face two demons he was well-acquainted with. "Elphior, Faustus."

They were part of Beelzebub's army, and resembled humanoid bees, with red antennae protruding from their heads, and beady yellow eyes. Red-tinged, rounded wings fluttered against their backs in an incessant noise.

"What happened to you?" Faustus asked.

leaning closer to inspect Daymun's cheek. He laughed. "Bit more than you can chew?"

"Something like that." His eyes narrowed on them. "Asmodeus seems in a furious mood."

"He always is, these days," Elphior said. "Especially since you won."

"How so?"

"Most of the horde up there are his. He's been left with few demons to harass, so he picks on the unaligned ones."

The majority of demons in Hell were aligned to one of the seven Princes. Daymun himself had never chosen one, though most knew Lucifer trusted him with assignments, even if the ruler didn't say so himself. To show favoritism in Hell was akin to stamping a bull's eye on one's back, after all.

And Lucifer, though powerful, would not go against the other six Princes. They had been in Hell long before he'd fallen, after all. And though he had been keen to assert his control over them, the line in the sand was clear—he kept to his side, and they kept to theirs.

"Interesting," Daymun muttered.

"What's so interesting?" Faustus shifted

his weight. "It's only the Princes. They always do as they please."

Daymun rolled his eyes. "Not much has changed in my absence, I see. Have you two already forgotten the true origins of our leaders?"

They leaned towards him, already hooked on Daymun's every word as he continued. "Way before Lucifer fell, the origin of Light and Dark stemmed from the waters of the World Ocean. You remember that much?"

Gosh, but these demons were idiots. Given their wide eyes, he needed to explain this to them, if only so he could get them to do what was required once more. With Asmodeus on the war path, Daymun knew he needed subservient creatures at his command. And the more, the merrier.

How easily he fell back into old habits of machinations already...

He forced himself to remain calm, despite the stinging in his cheek. A reminder that he answered to another. Something he'd lived without, for the most part, these last twenty-five years.

"The World Ocean existed since the beginning of time," he said, "and will be there forevermore, surrounding the entire planet. The end of it closest to Hell boils as hot as the underground, and some areas are cold, nearing the Kingdom of the Creator."

"Heavennnn…" Elphior hissed.

"Yes, Heaven," Daymun said. A quick glance around ensured they were still alone. If he was caught speaking of this, especially after his latest punishment, it would not end well. "Regardless, within the Ocean, the Creator and Nesfartatul lived together in harmony. Or as much as possible."

"Oh, oh!" Faustus started jumping and down. "I remember this! I do, I do. Nesfartatul was the Devil, and when he failed to harm the Creator as he molded his mortals, he got cast into Hell."

Daymun inclined his head, hiding his surprise. "Exactly."

"I…" Elphior frowned. "But I don't get it. Why the history lesson?"

Daymun took a step closer. "*Because,*" he emphasized, "when Nesfartatul fell, he cast his essence into six pieces. Each of those became the six Princes of Hell. Beelzebub for gluttony, Satan for wrath, Leviathan for envy, Mammon for greed, Belphegor for sloth, Asmodeus for lust... And, finally, Lucifer fell. And turned into the seventh Prince, for pride. And the demons who swore alliance to them, soon came to fall under certain categories."

Two pairs of eyes stared at him in wonder, as if he was the second coming of the Antichrist. Daymun held back his annoyance once more. "History lesson over. What this means is, now that we have access to Earth, the location of each Prince is even more important. Alliances will be formed, and some will come out stronger. *Some*, even, may choose to view Lucifer as the outsider—may unite against him. If you two don't want to become food for them, keep your ear to the ground and let me know of anything you hear. Understood?" When they nodded, he added, "So. Who else's army went up?"

Faustus was quick to jump. "Leviathan, Mammon, Beelzebub."

Which meant they'd dragged with them

their armies who fed off envy, greed—both of which used mental abilities to toy with humans until their demise—and, finally, those who preyed on the dead.

"Hmm. And Belphegor?" His demons were known for gaseous attacks.

A chuckle from them both, before Elphior said, "No. Couldn't get off his lazy ass."

"No Satan, either?"

If both Belphegor and Satan stayed behind, that meant the fire demons answering to the latter had also not all been on Earth. Not that it mattered, really. Humans were fucked either way.

Faustus laughed. "Why would Satan bother? He's busy down here, torturing the souls he catches. He figured he'd leave the above-ground to the others."

Poor humans. Daymun was shocked the minute the thought formed in his head. But realistically, they had no chance. Not against such a variety of demons, most of whom were ruled by the exact needs humans were.

"Good information, mates. I'll take my leave for now. Things to heal, stuff to catch up on. You know how it goes."

They saluted him and left.

By the time Daymun returned to his chambers, they were not empty. Fayana, a demoness he was fond of tumbling around with, waited on his bed.

Demons constantly indulged in the best of vices. Drinks, torture and sex were among the top ones favored, not necessarily in that order. But given demon hierarchy was completely paternal, the demonesses were always seen more as objects. Not that different from certain areas of the human world, in the end.

For Daymun, his fucks with Fayana had always been just an itch to scratch. He didn't care for her any more than another demoness. At the end the day, his purpose was selfish. Something he hadn't necessarily noticed before— and not something he cared to dwell on now.

Instead, his eyes roamed over Fayana's form. She had donned a human body this time, hiding her forked tail and regular olive skin.

Instead, a very pale, human skin glinted from the darkness of his covers, an odd contrast with the fiery ceiling overlooking her.

Daymun felt himself respond—she was naked, after all. And it had been a while since he'd last encountered her. Yet when he took a step closer, touched her raven locks, it was another's face he saw. Another's red hair. Another's touch he imagined on his skin, more wishful thinking than actual reality.

He took a few steps backwards, shaking his head. "Not now, Fayana."

She stood, languishing like a cat. "Are you sure?" Her lips kissed his jawline, his neck, and she sank gracefully to the ground. "I am yours, my master. And you have been gone so, *so* long."

He cupped her cheek, but the act did nothing other than remind him of Asmodeus' punishment. Not that Fayana seemed to mind his mutilated cheek. Still, he put more distance between them.

"I need to heal. Later, maybe."

She stood and walked away. Fayana was nothing if not accommodating. She would find her pleasure elsewhere for the night, of that he had no doubt. Before she left his room, he snapped his fingers.

"Yes?"

"One favor, love. Keep those ears of yours open and find out where the Princes are. And anything else you think might be of use to me."

She smiled slyly. "Of course, master."

The moment after, she was gone.

Daymun turned to the black mirror in his room and waved a hand in front of it. His burned cheek stared back at him. Half of the flesh on it had reconnected, but the redness was still apparent. It would take another half day for it to disappear.

Had it been a regular demon or one lesser than him, his flesh would have healed immediately. But a Prince of Hell? Their punishments carried more weight.

What in all hells was that about?

As he paced around his chambers, Daymun turned the question over and over in his head. His return should have been triumphant, not be greeted with silence and dissonance. Not met with punishment.

Perhaps Asmodeus had acted out of turn?
And if he had not…

Daymun stopped, sighing. His time in the land of humans had turned him soft. Eons ago, he would have been figuring out ways to dethrone Asmodeus. Not that he couldn't, if he tried. And it was a good move that he still had Faustus and Elphior in his arsenal, for the time being. But something had been on his mind ever since Katya's trials. And he was starting to wonder if there was a link to Hell, after all.

A Flama was meant to have only three tasks, to determine whether she leaned towards Light or Darkness, Heaven or Hell. Yet Katya had been forced to complete four tasks. And one of them had involved clear contact with both realms. It spoke of interference, celestial or demonic. And while her choice was made, and technically the whole affair was done… He couldn't shake off the feeling he had missed something. Something major.

She was staring at him with hurt in her eyes. He'd

betrayed her trust, her confidence. "Leave!" she
yelled, and he was thrust behind a barrier he
could not cross.

Daymun jerked awake. Hands were touching his skin, a mouth was kissing all over him. Fayana. And she'd brought a friend. He lay back with a sigh and blanked his mind, giving in to the kind of pleasure only two demonesses provided.

But when it was done, and his body was sated, theirs passed out on the bed, he was unable to sleep. He stood and paced the length of his chambers, his thoughts once more going to a certain redhead.

Why can't I get her out of my head?

He knew why. He had crossed the line. Twenty-five years was a long time to watch over someone, especially when it was a creature as complicated as Katya. And he had come to care for her.

Daymun realized he could have blamed the bond created between them. A Flama, by birth, had a deep connection with her guardians. With Katya, because of all the hurt she had survived, it ended up being an intense one. Both he and

Dante had felt responsible for her. They sensed her pain as their own, heard her thoughts when they obliterated everything else. They had had deep insights into her mind, perhaps more so himself than the angel…

How else could he explain, to himself if no one else, the role he'd played in her finding her fate? He'd had the opportunity to keep a distance. But he hadn't. Not when she needed him. Not when she called out for him.

And yet it was another who made her happy.

As it should be.

She had found her mate, Vasile. Daymun had, in fact, served him to her on a silver platter, and he had no business wishing for more. Sooner or later, he would forget her, he just needed the right motivation. For now, it was time to turn his attention towards something more purposeful.

"Fayana." His word, though soft-spoken, immediately awoke her. "What did you find out for me?"

"Satan's around, if you want to count him. Also Belphegor, Asmodeus and Leviathan. The latter two sent their armies up to hunt. Rumors abound that Lucifer himself joined in to oversee the taking of Earth, so happy was he with the Flama's choice."

Daymun frowned. The other two demons had confirmed much of the same. "Why? His presence will only draw the archangels, it makes no bloody sense."

Heaven's Warrior angels might be bound by rules, but they would not miss a chance to fix the balance of the world, would they? Or had things truly changed so much?

A shrug of a thin shoulder was Fayana's response. "He headed in accompanied, with plenty of arsenal."

"And why didn't Asmodeus follow? He calls himself Lucifer's right-hand man."

Fayana made a face. "He was otherwise preoccupied here. But…"

"But what?"

"There are other rumors. Of alliances in the shadows."

He stepped closer to the bed. It was exactly as he'd feared, then. "What kind of alliances?"

She shrugged, stretching against the bedsheets. Her lack of an answer gave him nothing to go on. Which meant only one thing— he would have to find out for himself.

Chapter 3

Dante

Ramona stirred from bed, untangling her long limbs from Dante's much darker ones. They'd stumbled in one of the chambers of the House the previous night, eager to truly greet each other.

Their nightly activities had lasted much into the early morning, meaning he hadn't gotten much sleep. Angels could survive on little, which made it even odder that he felt the effects of a lack of rest.

Dante groaned at the noises Ramona was making, then opened one eye to see she was scrambling to find something to wear. Whereas male angels were prone to prancing around with bare chests and jeans, the females still covered their nudity.

Watching her search for clothing, Dante was reminded of the differences between his plane of existence and Daymun's. The demon had been able to conjure anything out of thin air, his very will turning into whatever he desired. Angels could not—unless it was the celestial weapons each of them was entitled to, hidden within the coding of their wings.

But as for clothes, they appeared on whims, in various places. Yet they always remained clean, and their bodies never seemed to need the toiletries humans were so dependent on.

"In a rush?" he finally asked.

Ramona huffed out a breath, her angel wings trembling in both annoyance and exhilaration. "Of a sort." She pulled a swath of clothing from near the window.

Her demeanor only piqued his interest. "What is it?"

"You will only laugh."

Dante caught her wrist when she got close to the bed. He waited until she met his gaze before smiling, hoping it was encouraging. "I promise I will not."

Ramona let out a slow breath. "You recall that group of angels I spoke to you about, before your assignment?"

He racked his brain, trying to think past Katya, past the Hell unleashed on Earth, and back to his life before. Before... what an odd thought. As if somehow the previous him, and the current him, were two different entities.

But angels didn't evolve, nor did they develop. They remained as unchanged as the sky above. Or they were supposed to, as per the Creator's intentions. It was why Lucifer had fallen, after all.

Dante tore his thoughts from that and focused on what mattered. "Yes, I believe so. The Watchers?"

Ramona nodded, then waited. He arched an eyebrow. At least he could still read her silence properly.

"You joined them?"

A small shrug. "You were gone, and I grew bored. I know we are not supposed to, but there really is only so much wandering to do."

Dante chuckled. It had been one of the many things that drew him to Ramona and turned their friendship into more than just banter. She was impulsive and edgy for an angel. And as she was neither a Guardian nor a Warrior, she was prone to get restless.

"And joining the Watchers was your way of satiating that boredom?"

"In a way."

She leaned towards him, brushing her lips across his for a brief moment. It was enough to tighten his loins, his body demanding more than the one romp they'd had. But Ramona was already getting up and leaving through the wooden doors.

Dante leaned back on the covers. This return home had not gone entirely as expected, if he was honest with himself. The reunion with Ramona was great. But what really bothered him was Gabriel's welcoming.

The archangel had kept a close eye on him, even during his assignment. Yet Dante was a Guardian and born with free will like the rest of them. With a good head on his shoulders, and a distinction between right and wrong. Surely, he should have been trusted to carry the mission to term on his own?

And if he hadn't been, could it be possible that more was at stake?

Dante left his small chambers and returned to the outside. He envied Ramona, in a way. As a Watcher, she was able to keep an eye on humans—though, presumably, that was less fun nowadays than it had been.

In an effort to force his thoughts away from humans and what they must be going through, Dante went on a tour of Heaven once more. On his way out of the House, he made his way from garden to garden, greeting some angels and keeping his distance from others. Gabriel was nowhere to be seen, for which he was thankful.

Towards midday, as the sun glinted highest, and the temperature warmed, Dante headed into one of the meditation trees. Leaning against the trunk, he couldn't help comparing the smoothness of the bark to the roughness of the earthly ones. The gleaming glow of the leaves, to the autumnal glint of the real ones. The grass underneath his feet seemed more false, unreal...

With a sigh of dissatisfaction, he moved away from the garden and instead allowed himself to wander freely. For the first time in twenty-five years, he didn't have someone to protect, or watch over, or worry about. He was truly free in his movements.

So why did he feel so lost?

It took him a while to realize his footsteps had taken him to one particular area of Heaven—where human souls enjoyed their final rest.

Separated by a white fence from the rest of the grounds, it was also guarded by an additional portal to stop humans from escaping into celestial territory. The gate was similar to the Silver City one, but much smaller, almost inconsequential. Dante wondered for a beat if he could break it, then shook the thought off. Why would he?

He tried to make himself move away, yet he found himself drawn to the area even more. It took him a moment to realize he was seeking something in particular, through the fog he could see. Something like a certain redhead he'd been protecting for twenty-five years... Or, more accurately, her soul.

In the end, he allowed himself that moment. And a few others. But it was in vain, because no such soul was revealed to him.

Which is how it should be. Flamas wouldn't end up where humans do. They go to the Ether, their special resting place, which I have no access to.

With a final glance and a heavy sigh, he turned away and resumed his aimless walk.

Dante was bored. The original return to Heaven had felt like home, but was it truly? Somehow, his purpose here seemed...diminished.

Before Katya, before the assignment, he'd been guiding mortals to their ever-lasting peace. When a soul died, he—or another angel—was tasked to ease the passing. It was a purposeful position, or so it had seemed back then. He'd had patience of steel, dealing with the souls who demanded entrance, and those who were inconsolable over losing their lives.

In retrospect, Dante couldn't say he'd taken *joy* or found *fulfillment* in those tasks. *What odd words to be thinking of. Perhaps I did spend too much time in the human world.* Regardless, it had been purposeful. He'd felt he had a place in Heaven, a duty, and a set of rules to follow. An easy life. One that part of him wanted…and the other part was now conflicted about.

So he paced the gardens, paid his respects to other archangels and angels alike, and wandered some more. Lost in thoughts, more so than ever before.

Would he be allowed back to guide humans? Was that even what he wanted to do?

When Ramona returned, what felt like only hours later, her easy demeanor was long gone. Her eyes were filled with tears, her nose slightly red from crying. Angels, as a rule, were meant to be impassable. Yet here was one who was always bubbly, and she was a mess.

She found him on the edge of a garden, near the area Warriors used to train. Dante didn't even know how he'd ended there, but he'd been staring at their fencing and parrying skills for a moment when her sniffles drew him out of his ruminations.

Without hesitation, Dante opened his arms, and she rushed in them, more tears bathing his naked chest.

"What happened?" he whispered.

"It is horrible, Dante." She sniffled. "The poor humans... They have no idea what happened, nor how to protect themselves. They are dying by hordes, and the ones who are not are being used by demons!"

"Used how?"

"Half-demons," she choked against his chest.

Dante only held her tighter. Demons loved to breed, thus it was no surprise they were using female humans to do so. Not that their bodies could carry to term the pregnancy, but it would be enough for the demon spawn to form, and from there survive.

"The worst is some of them do not realize it."

"What do you mean?"

Ramona sniffled. "You know demons can take on shapes as they wish. Some of them present themselves as good-looking men, as saviors."

It was a trick as old as time, and Dante wasn't surprised. He was, however, oddly moved by Ramona's caring. Without seeming like he was doing so, he checked the area for a quiet spot. While *he* was moved, other angels would see it as a weakness, and it might raise Gabriel's awareness. Eventually, he found some long columns a bit to the side and shuffled them in the little alcove of quietude they provided.

"It is horrible," he agreed with her statement. "But do you mind me asking why it affects you so?"

"How can it not? If you saw what I did…"

"Perhaps you should stop." At her indignant expression, he hurried to add, "Only temporarily, until things settle."

"It will be eons before they do."

Dante could think of nothing else to say. He simply wiped her cheeks and held her until her sniffles had subsided.

"How does it not affect you?" she asked. "It was your…"

She stopped, but it was too late. Dante felt like he'd been gut-punched, and he stepped backwards. "Yes, it was my protégée who unleashed this on the humans."

"I am—" Ramona cast her eyes downwards. She could not lie with an apology she did not mean, apparently.

Dante sighed. "Katya had her reasons to choose what she did."

"Do you agree with them?"

"It is not my place to say."

"If not yours, as her Guardian, then whose?"

Her question raised more doubts about his lack of doing. His wings ruffled in agitation and frustration at himself for caring. Even more for his return being tainted by a choice he could not control.

Through gritted teeth, Dante simply said, "You should remember I outrank you. And my assignments are no one's concern but mine."

He stalked away before he said something truly ugly.

In the middle of the night, or what counted as night for angels, Dante left his room again and headed to the nearest garden angels spent their time in. Some trees were occupied, but most were empty. He chose one off to the edge and flew to the top, resting on a branch. He moved his gaze to the sky, to the parts still accessible to him.

The stars, the galaxy, the universe. Humans had it all wrong. They were so quick to discount possibilities and explanations for their existence, and to have the belief that one theory could not exist without the other. The Big Bang did not fit religion's view of a single God, and vice versa.

How wrong they were… and wrong that they would never get to correct such single-mindedness.

As his thoughts grew restless, Dante found it harder and harder to remain focused on the present. Not when what he really wanted to think about was Katya. Had she survived? And if yes, what stories would she tell him, when so much was left to his imagination? What truth lay behind the last of the events that had taken place under his wing?

If angels or demons had intervened, could the fate of the world have changed? Could it all be different? Would Katya had chosen differently? Or had he failed her, and humanity as a result?

Unable to sit still, he flew off the tree and back to the gate. The marble steps glinted in the light of the stars, both tangible and part of dreams. He was not under orders to stay in Heaven, but surely it would look bad to Gabriel if he took off?

Yet at the same time... Dante inhaled deeply and stepped down the stairs. The gate opened in invitation, and he was out.

It was a well-kept secret among angels that some Elders—archangels—chose to live on Earth in various strongholds. One such place was a monastery nested within the Carpathian Mountains in Romania.

Dante was familiar with it, after all he'd done some training there as a Guardian, and archangel Michael was an old mentor of his. It was why he'd taken Katya to him, to get her cleansed after one particularly bad trial she'd endured at the hands of a Dark Fae queen.

He recalled the place as a spot of peace. The monastery was as he remembered it—worn brick, patches of red and white paint, windows framed in dark wood. He didn't have to climb the many broken steps leading to it, and even from the skies, he could see the ground within the gates covered in cobblestones, looking worn and ancient, a fountain in the middle.

The surroundings, however, were a disaster. Trees lay broken, roots pulled from the earth. Some were smashed into pieces, some burned. Large areas that used to hold blossoming vegetation were now arid, ashy. And everywhere else, the scent of death and decay lingered.

Whatever Hell had been unleashed upon

Earth, it plainly did not touch the monastery, but it had spared nothing around it.

Dante landed in front of the dark oak gate, frowning. He could have flown directly inside, but somehow it felt like he'd be intruding.

"Halt!"

A shadow rose above the gate, darker and darker—a warning to anyone coming too close. But Dante knew better and saw through the illusion. He stepped nearer so the monastery's guardian could fully see him.

"It is Dante."

The menace disappeared, and the heavy oak doors opened. Dante entered, feeling the sacred barrier as he did so. On the other side, he was greeted by two very scared-looking monks in dirtied robes. A third one was in their midst.

He was older. Much, much older than either human knew. Dark eyes stared back at him from a wrinkled face—Dante knew the real features behind the illusion would be smooth, and the eyes much more golden than dark.

He waited until the other two monks left, then spoke softly. "Michael."

"Dante." The archangel shed the illusion.

His startling white wings, the color of pure snow, unfurled as he took his true form. "What brings you here? Your task was complete." He peered closer at him. "Yet something troubles you."

"I... Hmm. Has Katya been here?"

"The Flama? I have not seen her since our last interaction, over six months ago."

Dante tried not to show his surprise and failed. Time truly passed differently above, as it did below. "*Six* months?"

Michael nodded. "Yes, and it has been a hellish time since she released the demons."

"I have seen the area... I am sorry." When Michael simply watched him, Dante said, "I must ask, though. Is there no hope she would have survived?"

"Not many Flamas have, in the past. I personally do not know of any. To open either gate, even if they were born to it, is not an easy task."

Dante nodded. He had argued much the same with himself. So, why then, this idiotic hope?

"Would it matter if she were alive?" Michael asked. "Do you hope she could undo what she has caused?"

"No, of course not. That would be intervention we are not allowed. I had merely hoped... I am not sure what, exactly. Perhaps to understand. Perhaps to ensure she is safe. Happy."

Michael made a face. "Her happiness, at the expense of others?"

Dante could see how, from afar, Katya's choice could be misconstrued. But he had been by her side for the better part of her twenty-five years, and he'd seen everything she had endured. It was not a high leap to understand why she had decided as she had, though it was not his choice to defend.

"It would not be so. She made her choice for a reason."

"You almost sound like you agree."

"Not the first time I have been accused of it today." He sighed. "But I cannot justify her actions. I am here because of questions I cannot shake. Things that happened while her trials were taking place. Things that, since my return to the Silver City, make me doubt... Make me *fear* another's intervention... At least, I assume so."

"Are you referring to the demon guardian

who shared your mission?"

"No." Dante held back, hesitating.

What was he truly asking? If there was celestial interference, what would be the purpose? And what if Michael had taken part?

Too late to retreat now. He could only hope the fact Michael had not been in the Silver City for the last millennia meant he was not involved in whatever had taken place—if anything.

"When Katya left for the third trial, she was brought to Apa Sâmbetei."

Michael frowned. "The World Ocean?"

"Yes. As you know, the Romanian mythology is one of the few that still maintains some truthful elements of the original creation of the world, rather than all the machinations written everywhere else."

"A fact we all know. You need not educate *me,* Dante."

"Forgive me." He cleared his throat. "The problem is, when Katya landed in this so-called trial, three creatures the likes I have not heard of waited for her. They tried to force her hand, and from what she said, she was denied help from either Heaven or Hell. Had it not been for her own kin, she would have died in that trial. But she survived... Only to exit the task and land into yet another, with a muroni vampire."

Michael arched an eyebrow. "They are cave dwellers, nothing more. Primitive vampires, who can shape shift. About the only thing they are capable of, aside from murder."

Dante nodded. "Very true. But he almost killed Katya." He waited a beat, then added, "Do you understand my problem? Katya survived the challenge, but then landed into yet another one with a muroni. It is not normal."

Michael sighed. "No, it is not."

"It almost sounds like someone wanted her dead." Dante hesitated. The last thing he intended was to accuse Michael of holding back, but the way the angel stood, his wings now lowered, his hands pressed together in a praying gesture, made him wary. "You seem like you know something."

Michael met his gaze. "And yet how much I can tell you, is another story altogether."

"Michael—"

"I will say this. My position here enables me to watch from afar, but I am still an archangel. Meaning I am privy to the changes in the balance, the shifts that take place before anyone else notices." A pause, more telling than anything. "There *was* interference, but it was not only celestial. There are two sides to this mess, and both need to be held accountable. What I will add, however, is that the answers you seek may be closer to home than you imagine. And will require some hard choices, down the line." Michael glanced around the monastery. "I have chosen my fate here, and I will not desert it. The fact remains, do you think many others will do the same?"

Dante left the monastery feeling more conflicted than he had upon arriving. He trusted Michael to know these things, without being involved himself in the machinations. But what had he gotten out of his trip, other than confirm something hadn't been right? And what did it matter, now that it was all said and done?

It mattered, because he felt it was not the end. Not in the least. And regardless what he had been created to feel, he could not ignore this.

When he returned at Haven's gate, he was relieved. He had half expected Gabriel to give him a hard time, but he was not there.

Surprise did await, but in his room—in the form of a sleepy Ramona in his bed. Dante moved closer and kissed her shoulder, nibbling on the skin until she awoke. His thoughts too tremulous, he did as humans were bound to and got lost in the pleasure of the flesh, to distract his mind.

After, when they lay side by side, he tucked her into his chest. "Earlier, when you were emotional... I apologize for my outburst. It was unseemly."

"No, it is I who should apologize, Dante. I should not have let myself become so involved with what I had seen."

She tried to move away from him, as if ashamed of displaying emotion, but he tightened his arms around her.

"No, that is not what I meant. Why did what you saw affect you so?"

"Because… it is an entire culture, an entire species, on the brink of being wiped out." Another sniffle. "The demons are not being subtle, Dante. At least, not everywhere. In the larger cities, they have started full-on invading and enjoying the panic they cause, and how it makes humans react. In the smaller areas, they seem to toy with them. It is… horrid."

"But why does it affect *you*, Ramona? I do not mean to sound callous, but you had nothing to do with Katya's choice."

Ramona was silent for a bit longer, then finally said, "I saw her."

"Who?"

"The Flama."

Dante's wings fluttered in agitation. "When?"

"One of the trials."

"What do you mean? She could not have, she was in another realm…"

"There is another gate, one that leads to the World Ocean from where the world was created." Her voice grew quieter. "A backdoor into Heaven."

Dante froze. "And Hell?"

"Yes."

"How do you know of it? Why were you even there?"

"Gabriel asked me to watch it, I know not why. But that was when the Flama came by the gate and begged for help." Ramona wouldn't meet his gaze. "She then went to Hell's gate, for the same thing."

Dante was stunned. Katya had mentioned an angel, but she had pointed a finger at Gabriel, not a woman. Unless—

"Was someone else with you?"

Ramona nodded. "Gabriel. He is the one who said not to do anything. He sent her away. Dante, what if that is why she chose Hell? What if all this suffering I have now witnessed is my fault?"

Dante shook his head and pulled her closer. "It is not. Ramona, it is not."

But it was *someone's* fault. Not the angel crying in his chest, but the archangel who had overridden her. The same one who had overseen every aspect of the assignment and knew it well enough…. Well enough to sabotage.

What did you do, Gabriel?

Chapter 4

Daymun

His head wasn't in it. Not as much as his body, anyway. The fiery ceiling held his gaze, even as Fayana's moans filled the room, riding him into oblivion—hers, anyway. Her forked, red tail, that she'd chosen to showcase this time around, twitched back and forth as it always did when her orgasm was impending.

He should have been into it. Not that long ago, this was the stuff he'd lived for.

Funny what twenty-five years could change…

When she crashed over him, panting from her satisfaction, he pushed her aside, and got up from the bed. She watched him go, licking her lips. "Would you like me to finish you off?"

"Not now, love." He forced a smirk. "Why don't you scamper about and find us some entertainment?"

He waited until she sashayed out of the room, before dropping into an armchair. Even the surrounding flames seemed diminished, or perhaps that was an indication of his own mood.

This is rubbish. What the bloody hell is wrong with me these days?

He should have been happy. When Lucifer returned, he would get the welcoming he was owed, of that, he was sure. And it should have filled him with the usual amount of arrogance, the fact he had set in motion the events taking place.

And yet... Such was not the case.

Still naked, he stood from the chair and moved to a cupboard near the bed. Flames engulfed what was within—a particular brand of volcanic whiskey, gifted to him by Leviathan in one of his finer moods.

This, if nothing else, will clear my head.

He shoved his hand in, ignoring the slight burning on his skin. Once he emerged with the oval-shaped bottle, his hand was blistered. By the time he'd opened the bottle and poured himself a large glass, it was already healing. Even better. A little pain with his pleasure.

Daymun stared at the swirling, dark liquid. Leviathan had said demons of the sea created it in a volcano somewhere on Earth. He hadn't asked questions. For all he knew, it was poison designed to snuff out his existence for good. While he was a demon, he could still be replaceable.

Come what may, anything is better than this.

He chugged the glass back, followed by another, and another. At first, he felt nothing. Only the usual sensation that came even after drinking human whiskey. Then, it was as if something had turned the dial. The regular fire in his stomach increased in intensity, its scorching heat eating at his insides, crawling in his veins.

Daymun tossed his head back and roared.

When he next woke up, he was still in his chambers—still alone. His head throbbed like a band of elephants was sauntering on it, with a dull ache that pressed down when he tried to stand.

He leaned his elbows on his knees, dropped his head in his hands and sighed. Rubbing at his temples didn't work. He wished, not for the first time, that he had icing powers as some demons did. Instead, the fire he drew his strength from would be of no help to him.

Demons don't get hungover.

Oddly, what was in his mind was the night he'd chased down Katya's attackers. Before the quest, before the trials, before she'd made her choice, she had simply been a human female. A weak, human female, easy prey for those always lying in wait.

They had attacked her in an alleyway, and no one had come to her aid. He had watched alongside Dante, unable to do anything. Held back by rules older than them, older than humanity itself. Rules that forbade direct interference, unless their charge specifically demanded them to. Hard to do, when said charge had no idea they'd existed for the better part of her life.

And then Katya had called out to him. Just like that, his chains were broken, and he acted immediately. After taking care of her beaten up form, he asked her what she wished. He couldn't tell her what to do, to seek revenge, but he didn't need to. She looked at him, all full of vulnerability and revenge and a desire to inflict raw, utter pain... And said, *I want their blood.*

He had carried out her will with no shame, no holding back. Even now, he could hear the screams of the humans as he ripped their throats out, hear their agonized groans as he pulled out their intestines and watched them slowly bleed to death.

Did Katya realize what he had done? No. Had she guessed? Probably.

It was the first time in all his eons of

existence that he had acted out of a desire to protect. To harm, but on behalf of someone else. And it had been the beginning of the end for him, given Asmodeus had been keeping a close eye on him.

Did that mean he regretted it? No.

Then why did this fire drink bring it all up, when it was meant to make me forget?

Easy. Because he couldn't forget—not his connection with Katya, not the fact he'd never acted on it, nor the fact he would always wonder what could have been.

He got off the ground and poured himself another glass. Fail once, try again.

Get over yourself. She's back in the Ether by now. And humanity's dealing with her choice.

Guilt was not an emotion known to demons. Least of all himself. Until being assigned to Katya by Lucifer himself, he'd been a free demon.

Only a millennium old, it meant he hadn't yet chosen allegiance, and his primary purpose had been to corrupt mortals. Every few weeks—or months, depending on his mood—he picked some poor area of Earth and wandered in, under disguise, of course. And he would toy with humans, playing on their emotions, nudging them in the way of their darker impulses. He'd caused marriages to fall apart, parents to cast away their own children, criminals to act on their impulses... And worse things, too. He'd caused death more than once.

Yet through it all, aside from the need to ply a mind to his liking, he'd never even been interested in the humans' lives, let alone their suffering. So how come he could not get it out of his head now?

He gulped a few more drinks. And then a few more.

The party was in full swing. In true demon lore, there was a balanced amount of torture and sex, blood and gore, and those in charge were enjoying themselves. Some more than others.

Faustus and Elphior were front and center, entertaining a group of similar demons with their antics, and showing off a prized possession—their collection of human teeth. The fresh metallic scent Daymun picked up even across the distance implied they'd been out hunting recently.

He tore his gaze away from them, instead noticing the contrast in the setting. The cave was tall, over ten feet high. Smooth walls showed recent carvings with odd demon swirls. They had set the area up to mimic a human night club, with disco-like balls of light flickering above them in numerous colors— and shooting fire every once in a while. Because why not?

Creatures gyrated on the dance floor, or rather, separate dance floors permeated with sulfuric gases, and the occasional scent of something charred. Instead of tables, earth demons had coerced the cave to extend bits of benches to sit on, or forcefully dug into the walls to create little alcoves. Wherever the eye fell, surfaces were filled with foods—and humans, for the monsters who partook in such things—and drinks.

More volcanic whiskey. Perfect.

For all intents and purposes, it looked like

the court of a king, only set in Hell. But the king was absent, and Daymun again wondered why Lucifer had risked going on Earth, when he was so much safer in Hell.

Daymun found himself in a corner, surrounded by his usual entourage, yet not truly partaking in anything. The drink still tasted ashy in his mouth, and he deflated. Just being around all this was enough to bring back the headache. Pretending it was the fault of the fire liquor was easier than not.

Fayana noticed this and made her way towards him, sashaying through the crowd and dropping on his lap. "Why the sour mood?"

He held back his annoyance. Just because he'd accepted her back in his bed didn't mean he needed her around him every damn time he was out and about. But like most demons, he knew the uses of having a demoness on his side—to be kept informed—and bit back his nasty retort.

"No sour mood, love." He gulped more from the bottle. If nothing else, it did dull his thoughts. *I'll have to thank Leviathan.* Out loud, he said, "Just enjoying the show."

"Ooh, you always enjoyed that."

She bent over to lick his earlobe, but he felt nothing. Not a single tingle of desire, let alone the urge to return the kiss. *Still, appearances must...* Biting back a sigh, Daymun turned his head to own her mouth, sliding his hand through her snake-like locks to grip them tightly. She squirmed on his lap, enjoying the embrace more than he was, but he stopped just short of her getting too aroused.

With a hard yank on her hair, he pulled away and caught her gaze. "Do *not* interrupt my view." There was enough threat in his voice for her to take him seriously.

And she did... for a few moments. Then she spoke again, her whiny voice trying to lure his attention to her. "They say you should be master, at the same rank as Asmodeus."

Daymun snorted. "Who says? Never mind. Whoever it is, they had best hope Asmodeus hears nothing."

"But you did so well! Even if the Flama supposedly survived, surely Lucifer will reward you when he's back."

Despite all the surrounding noise, all Daymun heard was the middle portion of her sentence. Everything else dulled, becoming background fodder, as the words registered— *even if the Flama supposedly survived.*

He turned his full attention to Fayana, gripping her by the neck. Her eyes widened.

"What did you say about the Flama?"

"She s-survived."

Movement in his periphery warned he was attracting attention. Demons always loved a good discipline, but it was not in his best interests to continue.

He dropped his hand, allowing Fayana to breathe. "Who says?"

"Rumors."

"*Who?*"

She bit her lip, then whispered the name. He wasn't falling for the innocent act. Fayana lived for drama. It was what made her the perfect snake. But if her information was true…

Daymun tried to ignore the increase of his heartbeat. He was no silly human. He stood and headed to a corner of demons. He recognized one of them—a top soldier in Beelzebub's army.

"Krynos. What are these rumors you're spreading around?"

The man smirked. "Don't know what you mean."

Daymun leaned over the table, letting the full force of his demonic power rise to the surface. The heat of fire rolled through him, filling his hands. Their hue reddened, and the glass top sizzled and fogged under the pressure. His aura shone blood red, his eyes blazed, and his palms finally lit up with blazing fury.

"Tell me. Now."

The demon glanced around, saw he was outnumbered, and bowed his head. "There have been sightings of the Flama in the woods."

"Where?"

"Near the fortress."

It can only be Poenari Fortress... Our stronghold while the trials were taking place.

He turned to leave, but Asmodeus barred his path. "Something interesting catch your eye?"

Daymun growled. "Move."

"Is that any way to speak to one of your Princes?"

Despite the demon's cool tone, and the warning in his eyes, Daymun smirked. *I'm not about to back down to this wanker again.* His cheek still throbbed from his previous punishment, but he was willing to risk a thousand more. "But you are not *my* Prince. If I was ever to align myself with anybody, you would be the last demon I would consider."

Asmodeus moved closer, but Daymun evaded the attack. Instead of lounging around to return the blow, and waste even more time, he kept going down the dark hallway. He'd deal with the aftereffects of what had just happened later.

If Katya was alive, he would find her.

Out of all the places he had visited while on business, Romania had spoken to him more than any other. The dense woods, filled with wilderness, the scent of earth and trees and freedom in the air—that, more than anything, ruled his desire to return. Perhaps to even spend more time there. It would have been a pleasant change from the oppression and humidity of Hell.

But when he materialized in the forest near Poenari Fortress, all had changed. While before the vastness spoke of protection and sacred ground, now the scent of fear and dread emanated from it.

He turned slowly in a circle, peering at the destruction. The broken tree trunks, the burned patches of forest, the cloudy sky no longer illuminating anything.

Should've stayed the hell away.

But he couldn't have, no matter how much he would have tried to.

He pivoted some more, taking in his surroundings and making sure he was alone, before dropping to a knee and grabbing a handful of earth. He sniffed—more fear, more desolation. The demons unleashed upon humanity had done a good job. No way would their race survive, except for the damned whose path to Hell would be clearly outlined now.

Since when the bloody hell do I care about humans and surviving?

Daymun stood, pursed his lips at his mood

and dusted his hand on his black trousers. There was no scent to determine Katya had been there... Had he been played?

That, or she's already moved on.

Unwilling to declare defeat too easily, Daymun decided to head to the last place Katya *wa*s seen—by himself.

Moldoveanu Peak, or *Vârful Moldoveanu* as it was called in Romania, was the highest mountain peak in the country. At eight thousand or so feet, it overlooked a breathless sight of green valleys. It was also, incidentally, where Katya had stood to make her ultimate choice.

It took less than a few seconds to get from one spot to the other. As a demon, Daymun could dematerialize at will. All he had to do was picture the spot he'd go to clearly in his mind, and his body disintegrated, only to be pieced back together in the new location.

Though the transition was smooth, the difference in the two locations couldn't be starker. Whether because there were no humans around, or anything else akin to civilization, he could not make out. But no demons had entered those grounds. If he tried hard, Daymun could even catch Katya's scent.

Or maybe I'm losing it.

He was on his knees, hands dug in the earth, when he caught the footsteps. He turned, eyes narrowing. The human facing him had gashes on his face, some healing, some fresh, and two swords on his hip. His dark gaze was intelligent. Worse, it held recognition.

"Do I know you?" Daymun asked.

The man approached carefully, one hand on the pommel of a sword. Gave a slight nod. "*Da*, you do. I'm Mihai, from the Dacian village."

It took Daymun a moment to sort through the millennia of data in his head. "You're Vasile's friend. The one who tried to protect him and Katya with your magical tattoo talismans."

Daymun wouldn't have remembered that bit, were it not for his own reaction to the events. To mark a Flama was akin to staking ownership, and he'd taken it rather badly. But perhaps it was what had protected Katya, in the end.

Whatever the case, Daymun knew his mistrust of the man had also come from his own knowledge of Dacians. Some time ago—long, by human years, but not in demonic ones—the Dacians had their own kingdom. Much like all others that came before them, it had an apex, and then it fell. But at its apex, their high priests enjoyed blood sacrifices. Their intrinsic culture, their beliefs that death was simply the beginning, had fed more than one demon's fancy, even if it had not been on purpose.

"If it was so useless, why did you get so annoyed over it?"

Daymun growled at the man's taunt and then stopped. Tilted his head. "How do you know I was annoyed?"

Mihai shrugged, but didn't quite meet his eyes. And that gut feeling intensified. Mihai had not been around to witness his loss of control, meaning if he knew of it, it could only be through...*Katya*.

Daymun took a step closer. "Is she alive?"

Mihai said nothing, only unsheathed one of his swords. Daymun was under no illusion—the Dacian was aware of how to use it, and would, against him. Given the obsolete legacy he protected, it was quite possible he'd figured out a way to injure a demon of his calibre.

Best not risk it, then. Daymun held up his hands and cleared his throat. "I'm not after you to harm."

"So said every monster out of that hole."

Daymun's eyes widened. "You've been hunting them."

"Da."

"How long has it been?"

"A little over six months."

Long enough to wipe out a sizeable chunk of humans. Daymun kept his reflections to himself. "And you protect Katya, wherever she is, even though she unleashed this hell?"

"She did what she thought was right. I won't judge."

Odd, for a human. And it only added to his suspicion. According to the last of his recollections about Mihai, the man had a village. A sister. A grandmother. People he cared for. His friendship with Vasile aside, he should not be this accepting of a decision that had changed all that for the worst.

Unless he, too, had a connection with Katya, and understood her beyond reason.

Daymun's heart thudded painfully. Whatever his reasons, Mihai had just confirmed his hope. Still, he smirked, trying to hide his relief with a taunt of his own, designed to get more information. "And how's that justification working out for you, given your entire village was obliterated?"

A bark of laughter. "My people are fine, thanks for your concern."

The assurance in his tone took Daymun aback. It couldn't be—demons would have found them. They would have followed their scent, surely. Dacian or not, no magic could save them.

"Impossible."

Mihai simply shrugged. Something about his demeanor warned Daymun the human was not lying—on the contrary.

"Tell me where she is. All I need is a word."

"*Nu.*" Mihai pointed the sword straight at him. "And if you realize what's good for you, you'll stay away. Katya understands the stakes now, better than ever. She's done being manipulated, by Heaven or Hell alike."

"What do you mean?"

He was already gone, a blur disappearing in the woods.

Daymun ran after him, yelling, "Dacian, what does that mean?"

Yet there was no response. The human had vanished as easily as a sprite, and he was left with no further answers. Well, none except for the most important one—Katya *was* alive.

"I believe what he meant, is we all got played."

Daymun whirled around. For a moment, ivory wings blocked out the sun, but he would have recognized the voice anywhere after the quarter of a century they'd spent protecting a human together.

Chapter 5

Dante

Dante took in the demon who, alongside him, had been Katya's guardian for twenty-five years. He would have expected Daymun to be celebrating his victory somewhere in Hell. So what was he doing back on Earth? And why now, of all times, at the same moment he was there?

Better question is, why does he seem so desperate?

Though Daymun was dressed in his usual

suit, there were darker shadows under his eyes, and his behavior had changed. Where he used to be impeccably dressed, not a wrinkle out of place, now there was a ruffled quality to his clothing. His hair was messier than before, as if he constantly ran his fingers through it. And the way he stared in the distance, as if having lost something important…

"What are you doing here, Daymun?"

"I could ask you the same thing, mate."

Dante arched an eyebrow. "You are not still doing the stupid British accent, are you? There is no one here to impress."

"It's London English, thank you very much, and I'll have you know I'm quite fond of it."

They stared at each other like enemies were bound to, assessing, trying to figure out where they now stood. Gone was their temporary easy-going camaraderie for Katya's sake, and the sake of the mission they had been given. Replaced instead by what had always been there—a gulf, a divide as deep as the two realms they each originated from.

Dante caved first, if only because he realized

the way to get answers would be to give some of his own. "I came here to investigate something."

"The fact Katya's alive, you mean?"

His wings bristled. "What?"

Daymun glanced around again, as if expecting a certain someone to come out of the woods. When nothing happened, he muttered, "I heard from some sources she didn't die."

"And you believed them?" Dante scoffed, crossing his arms over his chest. "Because demons are such reliable sources of information." He refused to even wrap his mind around such lies.

Daymun glared at him. "She was spotted at Poenari Fortress. When I showed up, there was no sign of her."

"Of course not." He glowered at the demon. "Because she is gone, Daymun."

"No, she isn't."

"I will humor you. What makes you say that?"

Daymun tapped his foot. "I just know."

"Not very convincing, as far as proof."

"Forget it, mate. I'll find her myself."

When he turned as if to leave, Dante uncrossed his arms and took a step forward, frowning. He actually seemed serious. It was true they'd had a connection, Daymun and Katya. Dante couldn't dispute it. How much of it had led to the choice she'd made was another question.

"Why do you even want to find her? Our task is done. Did that human I saw you with twist your mind with lies, or something?" Unlikely, but he had to ask.

Daymun didn't answer, instead continued onwards.

Dante let him go a few meters deeper in the woods, before sighing and following. He collapsed his wings against his back so they wouldn't get scratched by the various branches protruding from the few trees still standing.

With each step, he thought of Ramona's admission that Gabriel had specifically ensured she'd been there, when Katya came to the gate. As if he'd known. As if he could predict what would happen. Despite all their other skills, angels were not omniscient, which meant the only way he could have been aware was if he'd been involved.

Was it possible, then, that his suspicions had some basis in reality? And did Daymun's presence on Earth add more fuel to the fire?

Daymun's words interrupted his thoughts. "Why are you following, if you don't believe me?"

"To make sure you do not hurt yourself."

"Rubbish."

The muttered word made Dante chuckle. "Not much has changed, has it?"

Daymun flicked him the middle finger over his shoulder, but didn't stop his stride. Every few moments, he'd pause and check the ground, then adjust direction. Little by little, Dante came to recognize the area. They had followed Vasile and Katya here, though it felt like eons earlier, yet it had been only months.

Lost in memories, he paused, not realizing Daymun had done the same. Not until he spoke, anyway.

"I need a chance to talk to her, just once."

The admission surprised Dante. They'd had conversations, sure, it was impossible not to, in twenty-five years working side by side. But confidences? Never.

"What for?" he asked.

"To apologize."

The words seemed foreign on his tongue, and for a moment Dante thought he'd misheard. Then he took in Daymun's slumped shoulders, the nervous tapping of his fingers...

"I will admit, you have me at a loss," he said. "Did you not wish for her to choose Hell?"

"I did. But not because of me."

A bark of incredulous laughter escaped Dante. "You think all of this was, what, because of a connection you two had?" He shook his head. "I knew demons are arrogant, but surely you surpass even the worst of your species."

Daymun's demeanor changed in a breath. He straightened and whirled around, clenching his fists. "Watch your words, celestial."

Dante chuckled again. "Daymun, I may be a celestial, but even so... I was there when Katya made her choice. It had nothing to do with you. Or with me. It was her, and her alone."

"You ever thought, idiot, that if we had protected her better, perhaps she wouldn't have chosen such? That's what I want to apologize for."

It hit Dante like a punch in the gut. He had been bound by rules to not intervene, forced to sit by and watch Katya be hurt, time and time again. It had been beyond hard, and not what angels were meant to do, after all. They existed to protect. To guard. And yet he'd always felt as if he'd failed her. He thought of Ramona and her Watchers.

"We did everything in our power." His low mutter was not as confident as he wanted it to be.

"Clearly, not enough, since she was screwed over in the end." Daymun's eyes narrowed. "Which reminds me of something you mentioned, as well. What did you mean, earlier? You said *we all got played.*"

Dante glanced around, awareness creeping on him—the woods in this area were dense, and movement was scarce. If they were to get attacked, he could not fly off. Daymun, on the other hand, would have no problem running off.

He pinched the bridge of his nose, trying to clear it of the thoughts. Daymun might be a demon, but if he had a problem, he would tell him up front.

"You are not the only one bogged down in rumors, it would seem." Dante sighed. "Only, I heard mine from the source itself."

"And?"

"I was told in her last trial, Katya went to Heaven's gate to ask for help."

Daymun waved a hand dismissively. "We knew that much."

"Yes, but there is more. It was a backdoor into Heaven, one that exists in the World Ocean. And when she arrived, an angel was there."

"None of this is new. Katya identified him as the archangel arsehole you answer to, no?"

"She did. But there was another angel, and she—I—we know each other, suffice it to say. And she said Gabriel ordered her not to help. In fact, he went so far as to forbid her."

Daymun's expression didn't change, but something about him seemed to tense. "And this source of yours is valid?"

"Of course."

"No need to sound so defensive. Just because you're fucking her, doesn't mean she is. They never are."

Dante glowered at him. "I would appreciate you keeping callous remarks like that to yourself."

"Whatever. The fact is, if the archangel specifically gave that order, that's because he realized what would happen."

"My thoughts, as well."

"Then isn't it also possible that one of mine did much the same?"

"Or perhaps Katya never asked for help. Regardless, if we were played for fools, I would prefer to be aware. The world is suffering, and this about more than her now."

"No, it isn't. She's the key." Daymun looked around. "And we have to find her."

"How do you propose we do that?"

"Before you barged in here, I had the Dacian in my sights. One of Vasile's friends, Mihai. If I could pick up his damned scent, then we can get more information from him."

"Perhaps. And if we cannot?"

Daymun growled. "Then we go to your archangel."

"We? You forget I am only a Guardian, as are you."

"No." Daymun jabbed his finger in his face. "*You* forget they chose us for a reason. And just because the choice was made and Hell unleashed, doesn't mean our mission is done for. As long as Katya's alive, we're in this game. Even more so if someone's fucking with us. I won't take the fall or be held responsible for something I had no hand in."

Dante was tempted to agree, for once.

By the time the sun was setting, they were deep in the woods. Dante kept glancing upwards, wondering if anyone had noticed he was gone. Or, worse, if Ramona had told Gabriel.

In an attempt to distract himself, he tried again with Daymun. "I take it they lauded your return home far and wide?"

"Something like that." He chanced a glance over his shoulder. "Yours?"

"Something like that," Dante echoed.

No need to explain just how untrustworthy he'd become in the eyes of the archangel, or how uneasy he felt to be back in Heaven. Clearly,

Daymun had no such qualms.

"Did you—"

"Shh!" Daymun lifted a palm, then kneeled, expression intense upon something.

A moment later, Dante saw it, too— a footprint. Smaller than a man's, and definitely no animal. Daymun reached to touch it, but a voice stopped him.

"Enough."

From the darkness, a dark-haired man emerged. Dante recognized him from the brief flash, earlier. *Must be the Dacian.*

His hair glowed raven-black in the moon's light, and his eyes reflected annoyance. Annoyance and fear. "You've followed me enough, but this is as far as you go."

Daymun straightened, shrugging in complete fake nonchalance. "Tell me what I want, and I'll stop."

"Us," Dante corrected. "Tell *us.*"

The man took in their determined expressions, then opened his mouth. "She's alive, as you guessed. But she's had it with this world."

"What does that mean?"

"It means she's done being a Flama."

Daymun snorted. "Right, human? She wishes to live a happily ever after with Vasile, pretending to be nothing more than some villager?"

"Can you blame her?" Mihai asked. "She's been through enough."

"I find it hard to believe you." Daymun's expression was narrowed. "This isn't the first time you've made the statement, seeming as if you don't judge her. Yet, my experience with humans tells me it's utter shite. So, which is it, Dacian?"

Dante had to admit he had a point. Whatever his personal ties with Katya, Mihai's lack of a reaction gave room for pause. It was almost *too* tolerating.

Mihai met their gazes full on, though. "And to me, it would seem *utter shite*—as you put it— that a demon and an angel would work together, long after their assignment was finished." He arched an eyebrow. "Perception is everything, my friends."

"Good points." Dante threw a warning glance to Daymun. "Perhaps you can enlighten us, then."

Mihai glanced between them, nodding.

"*Foarte bine.* What do you know about Dacian culture, either of you?"

"Blood sacrifices," was Daymun's quick answer.

Dante tried to take longer than a second and, more to the point, avoid stereotypes. The downside of Heaven was, in the time Dacians were in power in Romania—around 168 B.C.—he'd been young and interested only in Heaven's gardens and all the peace he found in them.

"I have to admit to my lack of knowledge," he ended up saying. "I do seem to recall you were mainly situated in the old province of Muntenia, around these same parts if I'm not mistaken."

Mihai nodded, as if respecting the admission. "Da, you are correct. Muntenia was our land, and though our origins are shrouded in more shadows than I care to admit, a group of us came from the northern lands, where the Celts used to live. As such, my people were blessed with many gifts. Chief among them were healing, knowing herbal remedies, and a certain understanding of the stars."

"The stars?" Dante frowned, recalling his own obsession with them.

"Da, the stars. We were craftsmen in many things, including bracelets, funerary monuments, fortifications, and clay pottery." A mocking laugh escaped him. "Not that you care about those, I imagine."

Daymun took that moment to roll his eyes. "We don't, not really. Get to the bloody point, would you?"

Mihai glared at him, then shrugged. "We were a rich culture. In agriculture, in ceramics, metalworking... Mining. Gold and silver were our coin, and we did well in trade. Doing *too well* caused our misery. When enemies started coming after us, our high priests turned to the unknown for help. To... *magie.*"

Dante rolled the word around in his head. *Magic.* "What kind of magic?"

"The blood-sacrificing kind," Daymun supplied.

Dante furrowed his brow. "I still do not see how this connects to your lack of judgment at Katya's choice."

Mihai sighed. "Maybe I misspoke, then. It's not that I don't judge her for causing the destruction of this world. I'm entitled to my opinion, and that I will take to my grave. But I do accept it. What she chose, *why* she chose it... It's not as different as what my ancestors chose."

"How so?"

"Dacian religion believes strongly in the immortality of a soul. We see death as a beginning, a change of country, practically." He turned to Dante with a small, ironic smile. "It's why we serve the god of death, Zamolxis. This may hurt your ears, angel, but I won't hide my beliefs."

Dante nodded. Oddly, the words did not offend him, instead fed his curiosity. "This god of yours... Do you still serve him?"

Mihai shrugged, glancing in the distance. "It's impossible not to." Then he shook himself out of his thoughts. "Whatever the case, when immortality is what you serve, the life you live ceases to feel so short. Had my village been obliterated, I would've gladly joined them in death and celebrated our new beginning. But as it was, they were not. We were protected. With that in mind, and knowing what Katya went through... Da, I accept her choice. And on some level, I believe happiness is owed to her at this stage. Don't you?"

"Yes," Dante answered before his counterpart could. He could not let this chance go by. "Of course, we do. We were there, this last quarter of a century, and we know... *I* know, the truth in her heart." He took a deep breath. "Tell her you saw us, please, that...we are happy for her." He stepped closer to Daymun, clearing his throat for emphasis.

When he spoke, the demon's voice was hoarser than before. "Tell her...she did well, and that I'm sorry. We will take care of what is unfinished. Make sure she has her wish."

Dante realized, same as Daymun, that Katya being alive changed everything. No Flama, to their knowledge, had survived the trial and her choice. Whether by the Dacian's tattoo protection, or her own resilience, she had. Which only made the extra hardships she'd been put through, towards the end, even more suspicious.

Plainly unaware of Dante's realization, Mihai nodded at their words and turned to leave. But he caught the sound of a broken twig, then many, at the same time the guardians did. He froze and backed away, but it was too late.

Cackles echoed all around them as an illusion fell. Only then did Dante realize they'd been watched, the entire time, by a clan of demons. They looked like hyenas with human features, their muzzles stretched into mouths to speak and snarl, oozing drool on the ground beneath them. White eyes tinged with burgundy stared at them, enough to make Dante shiver.

Once, he'd been taught the various levels of Hell's hierarchy, and the many demons under each Prince. But these did have any such characteristics. On the contrary, they were decidedly... evil.

Dante's wings fluttered, but he had no way of expanding them. To do so would mean getting them harmed by the trees surrounding him, and he could not risk it. Nor could he leave the fight.

"Did you do this?" he asked Daymun.

The demon threw him an incensed glare. "Bite me, celestial. I wasn't involved." Louder, he said, "What's the meaning of this?"

The demons—for they had to be demons,

with their ugly shapes and snarling noises—only inched closer. One of them took a deep whiff from Mihai.

"He has the one we seek." Like a unit, the rest of them closed in.

Dante tried to determine a pattern to their movement, something that could give them an edge. But there was none. Mihai unsheathed one of his blades and slashed at the first demon—once, twice, and the head came off.

"Mihai, toss me one!"

Dante turned to his right, where Daymun was close to being overrun by a pack of the monsters. And he had no weapon—why didn't he have one?

After a slight hesitation, Mihai did as he asked. Sword in hand, Daymun jumped in front of Dante and slashed enough to push a few demons away. Did he realize the angel was trying to figure out a way out for them?

"I come from the same place as you," Daymun roared, "and I order you to back away from this human!"

"No," the leader said. "We want him and the one he hides."

"Like hell you'll get her!" Daymun growled and chopped off his hand.

As the demon howled in agony, Daymun spun, slashed another, and then his head. Mihai was grabbed from behind by another monster—but Dante was there, tossing him off.

He turned the human to face him. "Stay between us. Once we clear a path, run, and don't look back. But make sure Katya remains safe!"

Mihai nodded, then took a fighting position, sword raised.

Dante took advantage of the other two buying time and reached for one of his wings, yanking out a feather. Though the stinging sensation was small, it was a warning, one he chose to ignore as he kept blowing on the feather. Agony spread through his body—what he was attempting was meant for Warriors, not Guardians. Yet he had no choice.

It's a good thing Michael didn't care about breaking a few rules when he taught me this.

The feather expanded, elongated, until in his hands was a sword. It glinted with a light not of the earthly world. The pommel fit his hand like it was made for it, the coolness of the metal offering a perfect grip.

Dante knew he had crossed a line. Weapons such as this one—which every angel had the ability to create—were not allowed on Earth because of how dangerous they could be in the wrong hands.

I have no choice, though. If you are watching, Gabriel, you had best take that into account.

As he contemplated the blade's weight in his palm, Daymun yelled at him. "Been holding back, mate?"

"Only a little." Dante offered a weak grin, then joined him in the fray.

For each cut Daymun delivered, Dante delivered four. The sword moved like an extension of him—it was, in a way, born of his celestial essence—and demons turned to ashes with a single slash.

When the area was clear enough, he shouted to Mihai, "Go! Now!" As the human disappeared in darkness, he added, "And may the Creator watch over you."

To his right, Daymun muttered under his breath, and a wall of fire whooshed from the ground. Its flames crackled and burned, rising higher still. A hint of electricity seemed to sear through them, ensuring any demon trying to chase after Mihai was stuck.

Only problem was, so were the two guardians.

"Think you may have overreached a tad?" Dante mumbled. He could fly above the barrier, but what of Daymun?

No answer came from his companion, other than some muttered curses. Dante took that as his cue to keep going, cutting and slashing through the demons.

In his heart of hearts, he tried to mask his tumult. No one knew he was on Earth, nor that Katya was alive. Yet these creatures had and, worse, had attempted to stop Mihai. If they hadn't been there, what would have happened to the human? And why would demons care to harm the one who had unleashed them onto Earth, gave them their freedom?

What are the chances this was all a coincidence... and not some other twist in this plot we have uncovered?

Keeping his thoughts to himself, Dante focused on cutting through more creatures.

But right as it seemed the tide was turning in their favor, he heard a shout, followed by some swearing. He turned—Daymun was on bended knee, his sword embedded in a demon's gut. But that monster's teeth were sunk in his forearm.

Chapter 6

Daymun

"Fuuuck." A low growl escaped Daymun.

Sharp canines dug in his arm, tearing through flesh and bone. Despite the sword he'd swung in the monster's gut, he didn't let go. His eyes bulged out of its head, as if to ask why the betrayal, but Daymun had no answer for him.

He couldn't figure out for himself why he'd chosen to protect Mihai, and even allowed him to escape, although this would mean he'd never get what he wanted—a chance to see Katya again. And yet none of that made him switch sides.

With a grunt, he dug the sword deeper, and the demon's long tongue came out, lolling like he was a dog in heat. Its saliva slipped and spread over Daymun's torn shirt and into his wound. He hissed at the same moment the air filled with an acrid stink.

Figures. A fucking acid demon, of all types.

The various princely hordes had certain affinities—fire, acid, mud, electricity, and more. None of which gave him any clue as to whom the creature belonged. Acid demons were all over the place in Hell. And if this one belonged to one particular Prince, he should have recognized in Daymun a counterpart and backed off.

Instead, he seemed even further incensed by the angel blood he could smell in Dante. Even with his fangs dug in Daymun's arm, it fixed his beady eyes on the angel.

Daymun twisted the blade, then yanked it out and pushed the demon off with his free hand. It staggered, then fell backwards, expiring at once. Fire engulfed him until nothing was left.

A quick glance around showed Dante

turning a few more to ash. That celestial blade came in handy, after all. Yet even as he fought their attackers, the angel moved closer to him, until he was within hearing range.

"Did you tell anyone you were coming up here?"

Daymun tossed him a glare. "Do you think I'm stupid?"

"Not at first glance."

After dispatching another demon, Daymun turned to face him. "I've got half a mind to leave you with these fuckers. See how you make out with so many of them." He was fully aware not all angels were trained in fighting, not like Warriors were.

In response, Dante shook his head, as if he was talking to a petulant child, then slashed more attackers in the air above Daymun. A demon head rolled into a ravine, only to be equally swallowed by bright flames. The movement caused the closest of his counterparts to jump at each other for a chance at being the next leader.

Daymun narrowed his eyes on Dante's sword, angling his body away. "Keep that blade far away from me."

"Answer my question, then."

"No, I bloody well didn't tell anyone! When I heard the rumors, I came straight up here. Out of the two of us, you're more likely to have told someone."

Dante folded his arms over his chest. "I did not *know* Katya could be alive. And if I did, what are you saying? That someone in the Silver City would have control of demons, enough to send them after us?"

Daymun scowled. His reasoning didn't make much sense, after all. But it didn't mean he was wrong, just that he was looking in the wrong place. "Something stinks here."

"On that, we agree."

Daymun didn't notice what happened next— was it the roar of the demon first, or did Dante push him out of the way? Whichever the case, the angel ended up extending a wing as a shield to stop an attack, even as Daymun ducked out of its trajectory.

A cry of pain echoed above him. He rolled to his back and glanced up. The demon had slashed Dante's wing, and silver, celestial blood coursed down the feathers in slow motion, and onto the ground.

As one, the demons stopped fighting with each other and turned towards the two.

"Fuck me," Daymun muttered. "*Now* they realize you're an angel. Mate, you've got to get out of here."

When he looked at him, Dante's features were drawn in pain, his lips tight with the restraint it took not to yell—and alert even more to come their way. The hand clenching his sword loosened, and it dropped to the ground, even as he tried to staunch the flow of blood.

"Why isn't it healing?" Daymun would have expected any of the Creator's angels to be blessed with quick healing, after all.

But Dante seemed in too much anguish for it to be normal. He gritted his teeth against it, holding onto the injured wing, the lines around his eyes tightening. Daymun couldn't explain why the sight of the angel in pain hurt him, but it did.

Blame the fucking twenty-five years I spent by his side.

Dante hesitated, then finally hissed, "My

non-healing is the least of our problems."

It didn't escape Daymun's notice that he avoided the question. Still, he glanced around. The demons were pushing past his wall of fire, clawing at the flames and some simply walking through. The fact he was higher ranked than them was the only thing keeping the barrier standing and pushing them back out—but they were running out of time.

"We need to move. Now."

"No, you do. You must leave me and figure out what we missed the first time around."

"It doesn't matter anymore."

"It does. If angels or demons are messing with the balance, it matters." Teeth gritted, Dante added, "Do you recall what Katya said, in one of her moments of extreme agony? She kept mentioning the Enlightened Ones. We cannot risk..." He trailed off, the pain evidently becoming too much.

Daymun recalled the beings. To Flamas, they were something more powerful than themselves. Katya herself had said, after her second task, that Earth was in peril of seeing them return, and being at their bidding. Who, exactly, those creatures were—that was a mystery he hadn't yet solved.

A demon jumped on Daymun's back then and he cursed, turning around and yanking him off. It was hardly bigger than a monkey, but he tossed him to the ground and with a sweep of his hand, ensured the flames from the wall reached out and burned him, like an octopus' legs.

"Fuck this shit." He turned to Dante. "Come on, we're getting out of here. We can discuss the finer points of this—including the Enlightened Ones—later."

"To go where? I cannot fly away."

"Somewhere on foot, then. Until we find help for you."

Daymun ducked under Dante's unharmed shoulder and caught his weight. He tossed one more firewall behind them, then picked up Mihai's spare sword and Dante's celestial one. It sizzled and singed his palm, but surprisingly didn't turn him to ash as he'd have expected from an angel's blade.

"Hold on to this, will you?"

He held it out to Dante, placing it in his

uninjured hand. Hopping around, they made their way away from the remaining creatures, though their cries weren't that far off.

"Are you sure you know where we are going?"

With each passing moment, Dante's voice became weaker. Daymun couldn't see anything telling in his wound, other than the fact it was still bleeding and leaving a trail behind him. One that demons would track easily.

He leaned the angel against a tree, eyes narrowing on the wound.

"Yes, but the problem is we'll be easily followed."

Dante gulped, the sword slipping from his grip onto the grass. His forehead gleamed with sweat, and when Daymun helped him lower himself to the ground, he felt his increase in temperature.

"Something tells me angels really don't take well to fire, eh?"

The joke fell flat, only heightening the silence between them. And the cries of fresh demons farther away. Daymun frowned over his shoulder.

"I told you to leave me behind."

"And I said it's out of the question, mate."

"Why?"

"Call me a traitor, but after twenty-five years at your side, I won't let you die at the hands of my kin. Even if you're a fucking celestial."

Dante's startled chuckle came out weak. In the distance, they could hear growls and snarls from the demons, as well as trees being torn apart and hitting the ground.

Daymun turned his attention back to bleeding angel. "On a normal basis, if a demon hurts you, the wound would heal, correct?"

Dante gritted his teeth, mumbling an answer.

"So once we figure out what's wrong with this, it'll heal?"

"Yes…"

He moved closer, lifting a hand. "Then this should be fine."

He didn't wait for permission, instead pulling forth on his fire element and shooting a small ball of fire, barely bigger than a butterfly, onto Dante's wing. The area around the wound immediately caught ablaze, and Dante opened his mouth to shout in pain. Daymun was quick to press his hand over him, stopping the cry before it had formed.

Dante trashed against the tree, closing his eyes in pain, his uninjured wing fluttering. His groan of agony reverberated against Daymun's palm, reminding him just why, specifically, angels and demons didn't interact much, nor did they use their powers onto each other.

A few moments later, the fire sizzled out, and the area was cauterized. The feathers around were burned, now showing a dark blob on an otherwise ivory canvas. Daymun moved back, releasing the angel.

"You—" Dante stopped, panting, and stared at the wound.

Daymun shrugged and pointed to the sword lying on the ground. "Time to keep going. You can kill me later."

Dante shook his head, but accepted his help as they headed deeper into the woods. This time, each painful step away meant they heard the demons less and less. Daymun's relief was nearly palpable, given he still hadn't figured out what he'd done to cause a horde of those particular creatures to go after him.

"It worked," Dante said, a tinge of awe in his voice.

Daymun chuckled. "You're welcome."

Silence rose between them, but was soon interrupted by Dante. "If no one knew you were coming, and no one knew I was coming here... How did they find us?"

"What makes you think they were hunting us? They seemed to be after Katya's whereabouts."

"The part where they stayed behind and attempted to kill us, perhaps?"

Daymun shrugged "Could be either or."

"What does your gut tell you?"

"An angel, talking about guts? How novel."

"And yet you do not answer."

Daymun rubbed the back of his neck. "For what it's worth, mate, I haven't a fucking clue." He glanced around. "What I do know is it's about time you come out and play, Mihai. Unless you're afraid?"

When the Dacian stepped out from the shadows, Dante tensed. "How long has he been following us?"

"Only the last few minutes." Daymun tried to hide his satisfaction. He'd gotten a second chance to question the human, after all.

"Well spotted, demon," Mihai said in his thick accent. His narrowed eyes fell on the angel. "You escaped the attack, but not unharmed."

"And they're hot on our trail. So, what would you say to some friendly help?"

The man glanced between them, then nodded softly. "Fine. But don't get any ideas, I'm not bringing you to Katya's location."

Daymun grinned all too sweetly. "Of course not. Lead the way."

The way, as it turned out, was even farther into the woods, until they emerged onto a ridge. Chains of mountains and hills fell underneath them in a rough expanse of land. Parts of the area were burning up—demons on the prowl—and others wore the many colors of a summer's beginning. Spreads of wildflowers and dandelions, coating the entire valley in a kaleidoscope of vibrancy, completely at odds with the destruction.

After much maneuvering Dante around, they walked down the side of the ridge, to a small cave hidden behind massive bushes. There would be no way the demons could find them there, and it had the added effect of giving them a magnificent view overlooking the valley.

Daymun shifted towards the leftovers of a campsite, far at the end of the cave.

"No fire, *scuze*," Mihai said.

Dante lifted a hand before Daymun could lose it further. "No apologies needed, Mihai. We would be fools to attempt it." He grimaced as he rearranged his wing, then picked at the scab until the blood started flowing again.

Daymun made a face and handed Mihai his sword. "Thanks for the borrow. Now, I don't suppose you could do something about that?"

The Dacian moved closer, inspecting Dante's wound with an odd expression. *Probably awe at being so close to an angel.* Daymun could relate—after all, he'd been close to Lucifer himself, and had felt the need to impress.

When the inspection seemed to keep going, he sighed impatiently. "Well? Stop gawking at the weird color and talk already."

Mihai let his hands drop from the wing and rested back on his haunches. "You can't fault me for being in awe at this. This...is an event."

"Yeah, yeah. Sing the praises. It's still blood, meaning he's still wounded, meaning he can't operate properly."

"I am not a machine," Dante interrupted weakly.

Daymun promptly ignored him, focusing on the Dacian. "What's the fix?"

"Your confidence in my skills surprises me." Mihai rubbed his chin. "It's odd... Shouldn't an angel be able to heal himself?"

"That's what I asked," Daymun pointed out.

Silence grew until it became unbearable. Finally, Dante spoke, his voice defeated. "It is a common belief outside the Silver City. But we are not capable of such feats. Angels are not meant to intervene in human affairs, meaning they are not meant to get hurt. Ergo, there is nothing in place to protect us."

Daymun gaped at him, the wheels in his

head turning a million times faster. "Are you *shitting me*?" he finally asked. "You're telling me your bloody Creator just so happened to toss your lot on Earth, and all without the means to defend yourselves?"

Dante winced, his gaze on the sword lying by his feet. "I have the means. Only, I was not technically meant to use that, either."

Mihai tilted his head. "It seems an odd way to show His love, if you ask me."

Dante said nothing.

Another moment passed. Then another. Daymun was still trying to wrap his mind around the fact this particular angel—and the rest of his lot—had no protection.

Eventually, he pursed his lips. "I thought it was the type of demon, assuming they were with a Prince of Hell, in which case depending on their rank, their wound would carry more impact. But if it was not... If the wound itself is problematic, or if they were rogue demons, it would explain why it won't close. More fool me..."

Dante tried to move his arm and another soft groan of pain escaped him when the movement drew his wing up. "I did not mean it as deceit. Simply, it is best that not many realize."

"Not many *do*, I'll bet," Daymun said. "If they did, you'd have had hordes of demon spawn at the gate of your precious Silver City, eons ago. Why wouldn't Lucifer tell us this?"

"Perhaps because even he wishes to keep a certain balance," Dante said.

"Someone else doesn't, evidently."

Daymun turned to Mihai, arching his eyebrow, silently inviting him to continue.

"Doesn't it strike either of you as weird? That no one's supposed to know about an angel's weakness, yet someone did? And someone ensured he'd be hurt?"

Good points... Daymun moved to the mouth of the cave, overlooking the valley again. He couldn't stand still, not when theories overran his mind. Each more impossible than the last.

Behind him, Mihai said, "In the meantime, I can stop the blood flow in a cleaner way than a cauterization. But it won't heal, unless you have help. Of the celestial type."

Dante nodded. "Only my return to Heaven

can provide the aid I need. But, please, proceed."

Daymun glanced over his shoulder, watching as Mihai went to a corner and removed a block of stone. Behind it were a few supplies—a bowl, some satchels with herbs judging by the smell, and a spoon.

"You keep a habit of having your stuff spread all over the countryside here?" he asked.

Mihai didn't even spare him a glance. "My people found it best to have hiding spots, as many as possible, in case something happened. Clearly, they were on to something."

As Mihai prepared a paste, mixing herbs Daymun could not identify, the demon took a seat next to Dante on the cold ground.

"So, you think we were being hunted, then?"

"I do."

"And what, aside from your spat with an archangel, leads you to that conclusion?"

"Do not make it that I am alone in thinking so. There is a reason you helped Mihai escape and stayed behind with me. It was not to be selfless. Such is not the nature of a demon."

"Ah, no? Then, why?"

"Because you, too, have come to the same

conclusion I have. That there is more to this, and perhaps Katya was a pawn, much like we were."

Mihai came close then with the green-looking paste, putting a stop to all conversation. With strokes of his fingers, he covered the entire burned area. When Dante's cut was completely coated, he sighed.

"That feels oddly better. What is it?"

"An old Dacian secret." Mihai tried a smile. "I'm not sharing, not even with an angel."

"That'll be a first." Daymun snorted. "Do you two need a room?"

When Dante rolled his eyes, Mihai sat back, watching them as if debating whether to say anything. Finally, he stood, walked to the edge of the cave and stared outside.

"They haven't followed," he said after a beat. "You can relax."

Daymun let out a breath. It was good to learn he wasn't the only one worried. After all, none of them could afford to fight more, not now. And especially not with a hurt angel in their midst.

"It isn't only demons you should watch out

for," Mihai said. "Since Hell's gate opened six months ago, many creatures have entered."

"Entered?"

"Da. Some were on Earth already, but others chose to return. It led to... An increase in crime, to put it mildly."

Daymun was silent for a moment. By creatures, the Dacian must have meant the various dragons, shifters, Fae and other entities. The ones who, when humanity had taken over Earth, had chosen other realms to hide in. *Until now, apparently.*

"So, humans finally have to face their own shit," Daymun said. "Big deal." He found it hard to care for a species that was so keen to sign their own demise and favored their selfish side over anything else.

"It's more than that," Mihai corrected. "The balance itself shifted."

That got Daymun's attention. It was normal for someone like him, or Dante, to be aware of the natural balance. After all, their existence was based on being able to protect the one creature who could affect it—the Flama.

It was even reasonable that one of the creatures Mihai warned of would grasp such things. Each one was aligned with either Light or Darkness, in an effort to uphold or tear apart that same harmony.

But for a human to feel the intricacies of the supernatural, embedded in the cloak of time and space itself? The same elements that decided the world's fate? It was unheard of.

"The balance? What do you know of it?" he asked. "You are human, after all."

Mihai laughed. He turned, and in that moment, Daymun thought he saw something odd reflect on his features. He could not place it. He could pretend it was magic, and it wouldn't be surprising. Dacians were known for their powers, which they chose to use occasionally. But this was more. And it made him aware of just how much was lost of their culture, in between humanity's ever-changing landscape.

Keeping those thoughts to himself, he stood. "Answer me. You have a few seconds left."

"Daymun—"

Dante's warning fell on deaf ears as he took a closer step. He would get an answer, and if he had to get physical, it wouldn't be the first time.

"I know enough," Mihai finally said. "Enough to say that you're correct."

"How so?" Dante asked.

But Daymun had already caught on. "He means we *did* get played. And we were smack in the middle of it. Isn't that right, Dacian?"

Chapter 7

Dante

Mihai nodded, though he didn't seem afraid. When faced with a demon, he should have been.

Instead, he was staring down Daymun calmly, as if his friend was simply another in a long line of people he dealt with regularly.

Friend. What an odd word choice to describe Daymun.

Yet how else could he name the creature who had saved him and brought him to safety? Surely nothing other than a friend would do, in the end. The thought should have made him feel like he was betraying his kin, perhaps even going over to the Dark side. Instead, it felt right.

Sighing, he focused on the conversation. "You say we were manipulated, thus confirming my thoughts. But by whom?"

"That, I'm not sure," Mihai said. "But the balance definitely changed. Creatures that were on Earth now have more power. Those aligned with Darkness have found their weaknesses much…lessened."

The thought alone drove a sliver of ice into Dante's heart. Before he could ask, Daymun beat him to it, his tone evidently not fazed.

"What's that mean? Be clear."

Mihai sighed. "Vampires can walk in sunlight. Werewolves—the *vârcolaci* kind who exist here, and the regular ones across the world—no longer need the full moon to transform in their animal shape. Now, they can do it in the latter phase of the moon, when it's not at its fullest. Trolls used to turn into stone at dawn. Now, they can survive in the sun for the early morning… And these changes only took place in the last six months. Give it more time, a year or two, and the rules binding them in Darkness will cease to exist. Need I go on?"

Dante was getting the picture. And it was not a reassuring one. He should have listened to Ramona when she tried to tell him—it must have been part of what she'd seen when with the Watchers. All this added up to a rather bleak outlook for humanity's survival. Especially given most of them thought creatures to be a thing of myths and legends.

"This screams of celestials," Daymun said.

"What would angels have to gain from it?" Dante asked. And to think he was calling this one his friend. *Might have jumped to conclusions.*

"To look innocent while the world burns."

"I doubt it," Dante denied. "But I do believe they may be involved, if not in the way you assume them to be."

"Yeah? Then how?"

"I believe the archangels—Gabriel, definitely—would have expected Katya's choice to turn out differently. When I returned, my welcoming was... cool, for lack of a better wording."

Something passed in Daymun's expression,

but it was only a flicker of an emotion, gone too fast for Dante to read it.

He continued, "It is that which makes me believe there is much more to this."

"And the demons?"

Dante shrugged, wincing at his wing. It hurt less with the paste Mihai had put on it, but nonetheless was not the usual feather-light he was used to.

"It might help if you speak with Daria," Mihai said.

"Daria?" Dante frowned. "Surely you do not mean the Dark queen of the Fae."

Not only was she a ruler, banned to live in between the world of the real and that of Hell, but she was also the one trickster Dante could go an eternity without ever running into.

Mihai nodded. "She's no longer tied to her previous kingdom. In fact, one particular change affecting her is that she can move as she wishes between realms, though she maintains her old hunting grounds at the gate of Hell itself."

Daymun was gritting his teeth. "That woman single-handedly hurt Katya more than any others. It would be my pleasure to return it to her."

"No." Mihai frowned. "I didn't mean go to hurt her—I meant to ask her for advice."

Daymun snorted. "We aren't *that* desperate."

For once, Dante agreed. "We can find other ways."

Mihai glanced between them and rolled his eyes. "You really don't understand, do you? She rules the Dark Ones now. So unless you discover why you're being hunted by demons of your own kin–"

"What makes you think they're not rogue?" Daymun asked Mihai.

"Because judging by the way they didn't respond to either of you and kept coming to attack, they were very much taking orders from someone else."

Dante ran a hand over his face. "If we were to speak with this woman...with Daria...where would we find her?"

"And I thought I had stupid ideas."

Dante ignored his companion's mutterings and instead forced himself to breathe. The last time he'd been in this valley, it had been to accompany Katya as she headed for her second trial. She was never quite the same, after. Daria, the Dark queen of Fae, had caused her to see the worst humanity had to offer, and his Flama protégée had fallen hook, line and sinker for it.

Are we about to meet the same fate?

Already, his body betrayed him. The Darkness made it hard to move closer, weighing on him with each step. Angels, being as pure as they were, had a rough time being around solely Dark enclosures. Daria's was one such place, and Dante wasn't sure if he could go on.

Daymun, much farther ahead, had slowed down. "I can do this on my own, you know."

"I do not trust you not to kill her."

Daymun rolled his eyes and shifted his body to hide Mihai's sword—he'd borrowed it yet again—but didn't deny his murderous rage. It was interesting to see how much more vocal he was about Katya's well-being, now that she was far from either of them. Perhaps that connection had always been there, but this time it was much, much stronger.

"Then hurry. Mihai said she would only be here until sundown."

According to the Dacian, Daria acted much like vampires did, and remained in her old realm until dusk, at which point she would come out to rule her Dark Ones—creatures who had chosen Darkness but had no leader to speak of—and hunt clusters of humans, among other things. Armed with that information, their plan was to wait for her at the mouth of the cave and ambush her.

Daymun noticed Dante was having an even harder time moving forward and came to a halt. "This is far enough."

"I can go farther."

"Don't be stupid, mate. No point putting yourself in a weaker position, when this'll do just fine."

Dante sighed, but did not disagree. After all, it was already dangerous that he'd followed while hurt. Before leaving, Mihai had cleaned off all traces of the paste he'd applied to his wing. Though it still stung, the wound itself had healed nicer than Daymun's half-assed cauterization. Already, a faint fluff of ivory feathers was growing over the patch, but Dante had a notion he would forever feel that pain.

Whichever the case, it was essential Daria didn't realize just how badly he'd been harmed. If demons were so keen for his blood, someone like her... He shuddered to think what she would do. And if she were to get it, what she could do with it. Dark magic fueled by blood sacrifices was still a thing, and its potency must have increased if the balance shifted. So while he walked, Dante kept his wings firmly folded on his back, hiding the wound he had no wish to reveal.

It had taken them the better part of a day to make their way to the lair. What with Dante being unable to pass through Daymun's portal because it was demonic magic, or fly, they'd had no choice but to walk as humans.

Now the sun was setting again. They crouched down behind some large bushes, in a spot with perfect eyesight from the cave. And it didn't take long.

Daria came out only a few minutes after

night set in, as if she had been waiting right at the entrance of the cave. Dante frowned, taking in her appearance. Her pale, blonde hair fell to her back in tangled strands, and she wore some sort of ripped gown. Her wings— he shuddered. They were not the shape of regular butterfly wings, but rather like bats. Edgy, dark, and completely at odds with her Fae delicate beauty. She waved a hand around, and even from afar Dante saw the black tips of her nails, as if she'd been raking the earth itself.

The movement drew others from the shadows—two guards. Unlike Daria, there was nothing beautiful about them. Smaller than her, but definitely male, they had dark wings. Similar to Daria, theirs were also pointy towards the top, like triangles, and their skin glowed, but of a sickly green hue. Pale gray eyes peered from afar, assessing.

The moment Daria moved away from the cave, Daymun whooshed his hand and fire engulfed the entrance behind her. Daria's guards flew out of the way, but she only turned and stared. Then, she twirled in a circle, taking in her surroundings.

"Who goes there?" Her voice was pure, bitter honey. Underneath it, there was a small waver, enough to be noticeable. When no one answered, she continued more strongly, "I will gut you and feed your entrails to you, if you do not show yourself."

Despite her words, Dante peered closer and saw her fear. It was in the shaking of her hands, the slight tremble of her wings that could be blamed on the wind. But he, too, had wings, and he was aware more than most how they betrayed his emotions.

It seemed he was not alone in his perceptiveness, as he caught Daymun's muttered curse. But what would Daria have to fear in this new world that was all in her favor?

Daymun came out of the shadows, followed by Dante.

"Brave words, for someone so afraid."

Daria's eyes narrowed on the demon, but when they landed on Dante, she stepped backwards. It was his turn to be surprised, though he tried to mask it. Why did she fear one angel?

Her guards inched closer, bypassing the

wall of fire and landing on either side of her. Their presence seemed to boost Daria's confidence, as she straightened her spine and lifted her chin in the air. At the same time, she held up a hand to her two companions, a silent instruction to stay out of the conversation.

"I am not afraid," she said.

Daymun only grinned, waiting, in that unnerving way he had.

It had the desired effect. Daria first touched the amber necklace at her neck, playing with it nervously, before asking, "What do you want?"

"We come in peace," Dante said.

"I doubt that." Louder, she added to Daymun, "Last I heard of you, demon, you had trespassed upon my land to retrieve your precious Flama. You should be thankful I never hunted you down for that punishment I owe you. Do not test me."

Daymun's stance changed. "Don't test *me*, fool."

Dante figured that was as good a moment as any to step in and cleared his throat. "We are here for information. About what is happening, and what you know."

"Why would I give you anything?"

"Because you owe us. For letting you live, after what you did to Katya. For not destroying the very realm you so love."

She laughed. "No. But *you* will owe *me*, if I have my way. Very well. What is it you wish to learn?"

They shared a glance. Did they really want to enter a bargain with someone so evil, and for a favor they would not know until it came due?

Dante nodded. He hated it, but the price would be worth it, if it meant they would stop what was happening, and gained more knowledge of who was pulling the strings. After all, between him and Daymun, they'd be prepared to meet whatever price Daria demanded.

Dante shifted his stance, trying not to wince at the pain in his wing. "Start with Katya. We know someone interfered with her trials."

"Your Flama never had a chance. By the time she was born, she had entered a world rife with conflict and crime."

"You made sure to remind her of it," Daymun hissed.

Daria shrugged. "I only showed her what she already knew. You should be less worried about me, and more about the unseen battle you two seem to have missed."

They had been busy with Katya, but Dante was fairly certain they hadn't missed anything of importance. Not back then, anyway.

"Such as?"

She ignored him, instead focusing on Daymun. "Before all this, before the demons came out... Did you not notice your demon hordes growing restless?"

"Yeah, as they're keen to do every now and then. But I had my hands busy enough with Katya."

"I bet," Daria chuckled darkly. "But something was riling them up, even back then. The balance being tipped."

"We've heard much the same, with you as the culprit."

Daria cackled. "I wanted it to be, demon, believe me. Because I thought it would benefit me. Only, it has brought me only pain."

"How so?"

This time, she turned to Dante. "Your kind

were always too good at interfering."

Bile rolled up in his stomach at her implication. Had he been right, then, and the current state of the world was to be blamed on angels? Or worse, archangels?

Dante forced his expression to remain neutral. "How so?"

When she didn't respond, Daymun, predictably, was first to lose his patience. In a breath he was onto her, grabbing her throat and holding her off the ground. With one hand, he sent chains of fire to tie her guards to a tree trunk, rendering them useless.

"Answer me." His tone was low, more a hiss than anything else, and filled with barely held back rage. "Or I'll drag you to the depths of Hell with me. Something tells me you won't enjoy it as much as you think you will."

Half of Dante wanted to intervene. Even if the queen was Dark, he had sworn not to engage in ruthless acts of evil. And yet, could this really count as one?

Then he noticed the fear in Daria's eyes as she looked anywhere but at Daymun, and something in him rose to the surface. "Daymun—"

"Shut it, Dante. She's going to tell me what I want to know. Won't you, love?"

Daria's eyes finally landed on him. "It isn't just a side or the other, don't you see? Angels and demons worked together."

"That's impossible."

"You two did, no?"

Dante couldn't make his mouth work, to get out the words meant for the queen. What in all hell was going on? If angels were working with demons, against their own rules, that begged one question.

"Why?"

"Because they are tired of humans. Like everyone else. It is time for other creatures to shine, to take control. Humans, finally, will be relegated to their rightful spot. Where they were always supposed to be—in servitude. To serve *us*."

"The Dark Ones." Dante shook his head. "But angels are meant to protect humans."

"And what happens to immortal beings after eons of seeing mortals squandering their livelihood away?" Daria asked.

When Dante remained stubbornly quiet,

Daymun answered for him, letting go of Daria so she was on the ground once more. "They think they know better than anyone else."

"Except a mistake was made." Daria twirled a finger, and a small mirror appeared in the air, showcasing three skeletal bodies. Dante recognized them from Katya's description, as they had been present in her last trial. "These are older Dark Ones—since before all else."

"What do you mean, *before all else*?"

Daria rolled her eyes. "They existed in the time of the original Flamas, and they alone can hurt them. It is why they were tracked down and killed, and these three remained. Hidden."

"In the World Ocean," Dante pointed out.

"Yes. Trapped there…" She trailed off, a wry smile on her lips.

"By whom?" Dante asked. He was getting a weird sense about where this was going.

"By the Enlightened Ones, to keep the natural balance. If Flamas were to ever try and overthrow it, given their massive powers, they could affect both Heaven and Hell. These creatures would stop them."

"That cannot be all you know of them,"

Dante said. "If the bargain is to stand, then tell us everything."

Daria flicked her wrist, and the mirror spun in the air a few times, until it no longer displayed the skeletal monsters. Instead, it showed Daria on her throne, with Katya facing her. Dante accepted the jolt at seeing his old protégée—but why was Daria showing them this?

He glanced at Daymun, who'd moved that much closer, his eyes riveted on Katya's form. Daria snapped her fingers and, as if by magic, they got the sound to go with the images before them.

"Long ago," Daria *was saying in the mirror, "when the immortals walked the Earth, they were created equal. Different, with unique abilities, yet equal. Neither was meant to rise above the other."*

Katya *said, "Like you did, you mean?"*

Daria *chuckled. "So you do have a bite, then. Good. But no, I was not the first. In that time, a group of different creatures mixed with us. We only knew them as the Enlightened Ones and thought they were the same as us. Soon, we discovered that was not the case. They were...*

so much more. Their knowledge was immense, spanning millennia and galaxies. They could shape shift, and see the future, and they warned us of things to come."

She went silent for a bit, playing with the stone around her neck. "Those of us who listened were awoken, allowed to understand past simple things. We were given tools to think beyond, to demand more, and to realize the mortals were a threat. But some remained ignorant and shunned the Enlightened Ones. Eventually, they left."

Her voice was filled with sadness, as though the loss was personal to her. "And when they did, the Flamas took over. Since they'd been favorites to the Enlightened Ones, they developed new ways to use their powers. They could cross the Creator, to open the gates to Heaven and Hell, and he did not appreciate that." Daria ended on a laugh.

Katya was silent for a moment, then gulped. "Where did the Enlightened Ones go, exactly?"

Daria's sneer conveyed how little she thought of Katya's question. "Who can say?

They overpowered all immortals, crossed any barriers or gates as they pleased, and that is why they were feared. Some say they lie in wait, just beyond the Ether of Flamas, waiting for the day they can return here and wipe the planet clean. But no one really knows... Not like I do. They were strong, they were great, our mentors and friends. And now...we are set against them." She paused, and her face hardened. "But we are not strong enough, and never will be."

"I don't understand," Katya whispered. "Strong enough to what? The Enlightened Ones are gone, and now one of my kind shows up only every five hundred years to clean up mortals' mess. Probably as penance for rising above in the past. So tell me, what is it you want from me, exactly?"

Daria leaned forward, elbows on her knees, and smiled maniacally. Madness glinted in her eyes as she said, "Let them come back. Refuse your task. They will see our superiority, yours and mine, and allow us to join their ranks. We will have power the likes you have never seen, enough to free your kin."

When the scene stopped playing, Dante had also drawn closer. He heard Daymun's sharp breath intake, his anger rising in tune with his own.

"You fucking bitch!" Daymun snapped, taking a step towards Daria. It was only Dante's hand on his arm that stopped him from striking her.

All the queen offered was a small shrug. "She was interesting, your Flama. Of course, now that those skeletal beings are gone, there will be nothing to stop the next Flama if she goes rogue."

"Except for her guardians. Same as we were, they will be bound to the Flama, to keep her in line."

Daria laughed coolly. "You believe that, do you? Continue thinking so, angel."

"What is it you are hiding?"

She was toying with them, Dante thought. But not even he expected the words she eventually blurted.

"A Flama's guardians are not there to keep her in line, fools. They exist for one purpose, and one alone—to kill the Flama once she has made her choice."

"W-what?" Dante let out.

"You lie!"

"Why would I lie, demon? What would I gain from it?"

Despite his nausea, Dante inched nearer. "That cannot be. I was not told. *We* were not told that." He narrowed his eyes. "You lie."

"Believe what you will." She tapped her chin with her index, as if deep in thought. "But, then again, you have both had issues since returning home, have you not?"

Dante's wings fluttered as he scowled, but he was mindful of his injury, so he kept them folded still. "How do you know any of that?"

"Because I, unlike you two, observe." Daria stepped backwards. With a flick of her fingers, the fire chains keeping her guards immobilized were snuffed out. "Not that it matters to me, in the end. If this world continues as it has been, humanity will no longer exist. And the Enlightened Ones will return."

"Is that not what you wanted?" Daymun taunted.

"Yes." Daria grinned, but something in her eyes read false. "The more Dark Ones that come here, the faster it will draw them—the Enlightened Ones. And it is your fault." The last words were directed at Dante.

"How so?"

"It was your archangel who spread the word. It is why Dark creatures are returning more than ever before. They realize humanity has fallen, and they want a front-row seat." With an air-blown kiss, Daria started walking away. "I look forward to collecting my debt, guardians."

When she was gone, Daymun turned to him. "What the bleeding fuck?"

"I do not know. I... If the rumors were spread, my instinct tells me Gabriel had a hand in them. As an archangel, he has access to everything. But this makes no sense. I must see one more person—and I must do it alone."

"No such luck, fairy wings. I'm coming with you and sorting this out."

Dante scowled at him. "Very well, but you cannot enter the hallowed grounds I seek."

"We'll see about that."

Chapter 8

Daymun

As they reached the monastery, Daymun found his mood tanking. It was bad enough they'd had to deal with Daria and witness the rubbish she'd inflicted on Katya, and now…

"This is your bright idea, mate? To talk to some fucking priest?"

"He is not a priest, but a monk. And above all, an archangel."

They moved closer still, but Daymun caught himself slowing down. What was it about this place that was rubbing him the wrong way? The monastery seemed fine, with its pointed arches reaching for the sky, surrounded by an old wooden gate. The sun was up, the air was fresh despite the mix of burned and desolated areas... For all intents and purposes, he shouldn't be wary.

Yet, he was. And the closer they got, the more he was unable to shake it off.

"Dante, hold up."

The angel ignored him, instead going up the many stairs until he was at the gate. Daymun stayed behind. After all, he'd been told not to enter the sacred grounds.

But if they're so sacred, how come I don't feel the barriers?

For a demon, hallowed ground meant a certain blockage. Lower-ranked demons couldn't even enter churches or consecrated grounds. Blessed cemeteries, too. Higher-ranked demons such as himself had more leeway, but only to a certain point. Such boundaries had been set up since the beginning of time, even before Lucifer had fallen.

No way they're now become obsolete, no

matter what else is going on with this world.

Daymun knew he should have been passing through some kind of force field as he neared the monastery. Despite this, nothing. Dante had already disappeared through the doors. Daymun should have stayed—he had been warned, after all.

But he found his feet taking him up the stairs. And, not surprisingly, nothing stopped him even then. No shield, barrier, or anything of the like. By the time he reached the entrance, he was even more perplexed.

Then he caught Dante's shout inside and rushed in.

Past the dark wooden doors. Across the worn cobblestone path. And then he came to a standstill near a fountain, in the middle of the courtyard. It was shattered to pieces, as was plenty of the inside of the monastery. Almost like a battle had raged.

Daymun took it all in. Then his attention fell on the two angels leaning against the remnants of the fountain. One was Dante, and the other was much, much older. His power reverberated in the earth itself—probably what had kept the monastery safe.

Only, now, he had gashes all over his bare chest, and one of his snow-white wings was torn to shreds. Dante was trying to staunch the blood flow while talking to him, but it was useless. Thick, silver blood poured like a river down the stones, getting mixed in the cracks with other debris. Like it was nothing special, most definitely not the life essence of a celestial.

"What happened?" Daymun asked.

"Come help me!" Dante's voice was raw, filled with pain. "Please."

Daymun neared, but there was nothing he could do. Even if he cauterized the wing, it would not help the angel. "You have to bring him to Heaven itself." Even he knew that.

Dante tossed him a glare. "I tried. I called and called, but no one will answer. And I cannot fly there with another, not with my injured wing. Michael needs their help—now."

"Forget it," the elder celestial said, grabbing a hold of Dante's arm. "Listen to me. A war... is coming."

"We figured that out already, old man,"

Daymun muttered. Why was he feeling sad for this creature? Angels were meant to be his sworn enemies. Yet he'd not only developed a friendship with one, now it seemed he'd learned empathy for the others.

Neither celestial answered his words, though. Instead, Dante asked, "What war?"

"Your Flama... was the beginning."

"We heard the same from Daria," Daymun pointed out. Michael started at the name.

So, even the old archangel knew about her. *Interesting.* Then another thought occurred to him. "Did she have anything to do with this, old man? Was it her Dark Ones who did this to you?"

Michael shook his head. "No, it was not." Then he shifted his gaze to Dante. "There is more to this than what Daria told you. A school of thought from angels... Goes against the grain of what the Creator wants. They wish the annihilation of humans."

Daymun arched an eyebrow, but held his tongue.

"But, why?" Dante asked.

"Because they took up too much of the

Creator's time. Angels were jealous." Michael inhaled a deep, ragged breath, coughed more blood, then spoke again. "Do you recall the story of the Impaler?"

Daymun stepped closer, not wanting to miss a single word. Months ago, when Katya was asking around, Dante had admitted Vlad Țepeș—the Impaler—a man who'd gone down in Romanian legend as the first vampire, had, in fact, been a celestial. A fallen one, much like Lucifer himself. His error had been trying to teach humans a lesson, and the Creator did not appreciate it. Forced him to fall. And yet, somehow, he had escaped becoming a Prince of Hell, like Lucifer.

"You know I do," Dante spoke softly.

"That was the beginning. He chose to live on Earth, sustaining himself with the blood of others, and delivering justice as he saw fit. Despite his fall, many agreed with his view. They remained hidden among the clouds, waiting for their turn, protecting themselves, to avoid the same fate. With each passing century, humanity made it easier."

Dante gulped, sitting on his heels. "You

are saying there is a sect of angels within the Silver City that envies humans and wishes them harm?"

Daymun wasn't surprised at his offended tone. He chose that minute to interrupt, feeling more than his counterpart the passing of time. Michael didn't have much left—and it was essential they got as much out of him as possible. "What does any of this have to do with the events of now? Or with Katya?"

Michael closed his eyes in pain. "There are rumors... of a banned species from here."

"More immortals?"

"No. They go by many names, but you have heard their latest. The one they are known by in this age."

Daymun took another step closer. "Who? The Faes? The Princes?"

"No." His beseeching gaze turned to Dante. "The Enlightened Ones. We call them...the Ossi."

Ossi. Like the Latin osseus...for skeletons. A shiver ran up Daymun's spine.

He was no stranger to emotions, as a demon he made his bounty out of controlling them for humans. But this... the way this decrepit angel spoke the name, caused him to be wary. More than that—chills of foreboding licked his spine.

"Are you saying there's more than just us at the top of the food chain?"

Michael nodded. "More... and more impressive."

"How?" Daymun moved closer, kneeling by the angel's side. "When were they created?"

"They were a failed experiment, much like the Flamas. But much more powerful."

"Daria said the Enlightened Ones—these Ossi you speak of—were more knowledgeable than anyone else. That they helped creatures on Earth." Daymun frowned, trying to put the pieces together in his mind, but they did not fit.

Michael tried to breathe, and it was a sound of wheezing and agony. He closed his eyes momentarily.

"Let me try to heal you again, Michael."

"Stop, Dante, this is more important. And besides, we both know the small healing powers you were given are no match for what has happened to me. They only function on your Flama, and at her request."

Daymun leaned closer to the angel, watching his face as he spoke.

"When this world was formed, the Creator wanted it populated. He created Flamas and Ossi. The Flamas were powerful phoenix shifters, and the Ossi were humanoid, but something warped their minds. The more they existed, the more powerful they became. Then the Creator made angels and demons and formed Heaven and Hell. The Ossi did not like this. They spoke with Flamas, incited them to violence. And then…"

A racking cough stopped him, spitting out more angel blood, and Dante was quick to try to rearrange him. Daymun and anyone in a five-mile radius could see Michael didn't have much time left. The question was, who had done this to him?

Michael waved Dante away. "Hear me out. Time is quickly escaping me, and I have much to say. These creatures, these Ossi, were sent away. Banished. But every Flama passed down their story from generation to generation, saying they had left of their own accord. And many believe they will return."

"Exactly what Katya said." Daymun remembered the words all too well, for they had chilled his heart.

"Which brings me to now." Another racking cough. Then he gripped both their forearms with surprising strength. "You must preserve what is left of humanity."

"Why?"

"Because as long as humans exist here, a Flama will be reborn to protect them, even against themselves. And the Ossi will stay away. Without humans, the earthly realm is doomed, and so are your respective kingdoms. The Ossi will come and eradicate everyone for their vengeance."

Daymun stood then, finally understanding. If the Ossi had been banished, only the Creator had the ability to do so. And it would have been in order to protect the humanity he had built. Which meant if all of humankind was to cease existing, the last of the barriers keeping the Ossi away would fall, and thus ensure their return to Earth.

"Why does Daria want them back?" Dante asked. "Why do the Dark Ones who exist here?"

Michael gave him an irate look, as if he should have understood by now.

"Because the return of these Ossi would mean a complete upheaval of the balance," Daymun supplied.

Distracted, he tried to take in their surroundings. One more question nagged at his mind. If it wasn't Daria who had attacked, then who? What had harmed Michael to such an extent? And why was he not receiving help from the Silver City he was tied to?

"Why aren't you healing, old man? Surely your station as an archangel comes with some perks, not like Dante, here."

Michael ignored the question, instead coughing once more. "There is no hope left for me."

"But why?"

He finally met his gaze. "Because Heaven will not take me back. Not now that they are in charge."

"Who?"

Michael never had time to answer. He gave one last racking cough, spraying celestial blood everywhere, and then his body went slack. They watched in shock as he stopped breathing, and more silver droplets coated the cobblestones near the fountain.

What an odd existence, and an even odder death, for an archangel. Immortal beings meant to live forever. Yet there was his friend, hurt by a demon's touch and still in pain, and now his mentor, just as easily disposed of.

Something stinks here.

Daymun glanced up, trying to avoid looking at Michael, but found his gaze drawn back to him, time and time again. His form quickly became the waxy self of corpses, losing all color and illusion. His wings bristled, feathers falling to the ground. And under Daymun's bemused stare, his entire body turned to stone.

He was about to move towards Dante, but the wind chose that moment to pick up. It was all it took, and Michael's remnants fell apart as if someone had taken a hammer to the most fragile of crystals.

Daymun stepped backwards, again hit by that odd sense. "Why here?"

Dante looked up, his cheeks bathed in tears. "What?"

"Why attack now? Why here? What makes

this monastery different?"

Dante blinked in confusion, his gaze not quite there, clearly blind to his meaning. But Daymun wasn't—it had been staring them in the face.

"These attacks, it's not about you, or me. It's about the places Katya feels safe."

"What?"

"The hill. The Dacian village. Now this monastery you had brought her to. Even us, ambushed. We may have been targeted, and not because of our affiliations with Heaven or Hell. But because of her. Daria said we didn't do our duty to kill her. According to Michael, someone else is in charge—and I'd wager it's that new sect of angels he spoke of. And if the places Katya considered safe are being attacked, as are the people who made her feel protected, it could be done in order to drive her out of hiding. Which means the next victim is Mihai."

When Dante still didn't budge, Daymun kneeled to his level, snarling in his face. "This isn't the time to grieve. Later, maybe, but not now. Get your arse up and follow me out of here, before we have another army of my hellish comrades to fight off."

Dante stared at him a beat, then another, and finally stood.

They made it halfway down the stairs of the monastery before being surrounded. Eagles passed above their heads, and out of the woods came not only a pack of demons, but some wolves with them. Dark furs, yellow eyes, their snarls echoed in the quickly darkening evening.

Daymun had seen them before—in a fight they'd had atop Poenari Fortress. They had defeated them, and they would again.

But the problem was his angel friend, still struck by grief, and unable to hold the blade. The moment someone attacked, Dante would be seriously hurt. And Daymun could not— would not—let him lose his life needlessly.

When the demons moved closer, he cast a circle of fire around the wolves then pulled out Mihai's sword, cutting right and left. These demons, whoever had sent them, were no match for his speed. And it was better that way.

A grunt of pain behind had him turning his head in all directions. Dante was on his knees, a knife of some sort embedded in his shoulder. With a roar, Daymun moved closer and picked up his celestial sword. It burned his hand, but other than the unwelcome sizzle, he had no issue holding it.

Right and left, he evaded, using the swords like extensions of his hands. He was cutting, slashing, only aware of the bloodlust pounding in his ears, and everything falling in slow motion. Even as he fought, his mind was way ahead of himself. To find Mihai, to get to the heart of it.

Finally, the last demon was eliminated, and the circle of fire had restrained the other creatures. With one clenching of his hand, Daymun watched in satisfaction as they were burned. Black smoke remained of their bodies and spiraled into the sky.

He wiped at his forehead, full of blood that was not his, as he moved towards Dante. "We have to go, now."

"No." The angel glanced up from the ground, tainted with his silver blood yet again.

"What?"

"What good has this done, other than create more chaos for us?"

"What *good*? There's no good in this, Dante. Only a dim hope to be right, and to stop what's coming."

Dante stared him. "I am going home."

"Home?" Daymun couldn't believe his ears. After everything they'd found out, he was ready to give up and return to the ones who might be behind it all? "The same home that welcomed you so coolly?"

"Because yours did not?" Dante's expression darkened. "Do not lie to me, demon. You were not greeted with arms wide open."

"I never said I was."

"Nor did you say otherwise." Dante let out a heavy breath. "I am done, Daymun. The Creator never meant for angels to become embroiled in the world's fate. That much has never been clearer to me. So, I will go back to doing just that—not being involved."

"What about what Michael told us? Does

none of that matter? What about the Ossi, Daria, *everything*?"

Dante was already inching backwards, his gaze on the skies. "It will be up to others, other than me, to fix."

"Un-fucking-believable. I wouldn't have taken you for a coward."

"Unlike you, I do not have an obsession for my protégée."

"Sure. Blame it on that." Daymun glowered. "Go, then. Return home and enjoy Heaven for all its worth. Until you get dragged down from it again."

He tossed the sword at the angel's feet, then turned his back on him and walked away. What was the point in trying to convince him otherwise?

"Back again, demon?"

Mihai glanced up from his pot, where he seemed to stir more of the paste he'd used on Dante. Daymun didn't answer, instead dropping his bloody sword on the ground by the Dacian's feet.

"Could've at least wiped it clean for me," Mihai said. "Where's your counterpart?"

"I think you know well where he went."

The Dacian shrugged. "Didn't want to assume."

"Then you had a feeling he would give up?"

"Give up... Odd choice of words. Is it giving up if he's choosing to preserve his life, and what he believes in?"

Daymun sneered. "It is, given everything we learned from Daria and the archangel Michael."

Mihai stopped his stirring and looked up. "The one from the monastery?"

"Why, are there others?"

Mihai shook his head. "Doesn't matter anymore, does it?"

Daymun walked closer and crouched on the other side of the small fire. It seemed now it was safe enough to have one burning, after all. "How much do you know, really?"

The Dacian said nothing, his gaze intent on the flames.

"Did you know about Katya, and us having to kill her at the end of her quest?"

Slowly, infinitely slower than normal, Mihai met his eyes. "I did. But you're mistaken. The burden of her death wouldn't have been on both of you."

"What do you mean?"

Mihai said, "The guardians representing the side each Flama chooses, they're the ones tasked with her death."

Daymun froze. For a moment, he forgot to breathe. "It would have been me, then? *I* would've had to kill her?"

Mihai nodded, and it was akin to a hammer dropping on him. How could he have, when he'd grown to care so much for her? How could he...

Daymun shook his head. "It would've been impossible." When Mihai said nothing, he kept probing for information. There would be time later, much later, for him to deal with his feelings. "What about the Ossi? The archangel said they're what we've been calling the Enlightened Ones."

Mihai nodded. "Indeed. I take it the monastery is no more?"

"You're bang on."

"And the archangel?"

"Gone, as well."

"Then it has truly begun." Mihai let out a breath, and it seemed a weary sound, rather than the simple exhalation of a breath.

Daymun watched his expression closely. "Funny. Michael said much of the same. That a war was coming, and the angels—or at least a particular sect of them—are in on it."

"They're not alone."

"And how do you know all this?"

Mihai stood, heading towards his backpack. As he ruffled through it, he spoke over his shoulder. "I, and my people, learned how to listen. You wouldn't understand it, demon. But think of it like the old ones who used to read the stars. We are blessed—or cursed—with similar aptitudes."

Interesting. Out loud, he said, "There's one thing I don't quite get. Why would angels want Katya killed, if it would mean the return of the Ossi? Especially given those same creatures would go after Heaven and Hell."

Mihai snorted. "That answer has been under your nose the entire time."

He stood then, with a piece of paper folded in his hand. Daymun's gaze zeroed in on it, and his heart started thumping wildly. But Mihai still had more to reveal.

"I'll answer you this last question. The restoration of the Ossi to their legitimate place—some would say—would mean an overthrow of the balance, a complete re-haul. Which, for angels, would equal escaping their life of boredom, and for demons, their life of servitude to the Princes. To *one* main Prince. Perhaps that gives you enough food for thought."

It did. Although Daymun felt that wasn't the entire story, but he would not stop until he found all the pieces of the puzzle.

He jerked his chin towards Mihai's hand. "What's that?"

"For you. She said to wait until you were alone."

He handed over the small letter, folded in four. With shaking hands, Daymun unfolded it. Katya's words were cursively written, with stark, black ink over the yellowing paper.

I am alive, and I am well. Please thank

Dante for me. And thank you. For everything you did. Though you think me choosing Vasile, and that tattoo, made me less, that it stopped my potential... It didn't. I've given all I can to this world. Now, I only want my peace of mind. Let me have it, Daymun, please.

He sighed and glanced up. "She's happy, then?"

"She is."

"And when all this comes to pass?"

"She might fight. More than likely, she won't. And we'll protect her, stand by her, as will her mate."

"Because you accept her choice."

"Exactly." Mihai inclined his head, as if hiding his own emotions.

Daymun rubbed the back of his neck. "And if she doesn't die, another Flama will never be born."

"Correct."

"Perhaps it's best this way, then."

With a nod to the Dacian, Daymun left. He waited until he was in the woods before calling upon his connection to Hell and preparing to return home. Where he belonged.

Chapter 9

Dante

His wing still pained him. Dante tried to ignore it as he walked to Vârful Moldoveanu, the highest peak of the land he was in, but it was impossible. With each step he took, he got more weighed down. He paused at one point, breathing in the fresh air. As night drew nearer once more, the temperature dropped a few degrees and the coolness cut at his lungs.

Enjoy Heaven for all its worth. Until you get dragged down from it again.

Daymun's words rang in his ears, over and over, annoying in their repetition. No matter how hard Dante tried to shake them off, he couldn't.

Should he have stayed? *Could* he have, even? It wasn't like Heaven was a 9 to 5 job, after all he had full disclosure in what he did or didn't do. But what would have been the point, lingering around?

To say Michael's death had hit him harshly would be an understatement. Something about seeing the archangel expire, and return whence he'd been created, had shattered Dante's illusion of immortality. Along with his own wound, it had made him only more aware of how easily he could falter, and cease to exist, as well.

His little side quest had led to nothing but trouble, and unwelcome knowledge. What did it help, that he knew about the sect of angels, or Ossi, or that he and Daymun had been meant to kill Katya?

It helped nothing. Not a single thing.

Nobody could change what was done. And, whether or not he liked it, it was time to return home. Time to leave it all behind... and announce that Michael had found his demise.

With a heavy heart, he turned his gaze to the sky, drew a deep breath, and pushed off the ground. It took a few tries to catch the kind of air he needed, but eventually he did and breathed the freshness wavering above all the destruction below.

Farther and farther from Earth and its pain he went, higher and higher to the skies above, and past the portal signaling his return home.

Soon, the gate of the Silver City manifested, and he was back at its edge. Just like before, a wave of something passed over him, and he left lighter. Somewhat. Not as much as before, but somewhat. Then he took a step closer to the doorway, intending to pass through, but it did not open.

Dante frowned. As the clouds under his bare feet changed to steps, he strode purposefully farther, but to no avail. The gate remained resolutely closed.

Something in him turned cold, colder than it had ever been. Angels were not prone to human emotions, not in the sense humans saw them. But in that moment, Dante felt the icy fingers of fear take hold of his insides and squeeze. His heartbeat picked up—once, twice.

A moment later, he slammed his hands on the intrinsic design of the gate. The metal was cool against his palms, but nothing happened. "Open!"

He banged again.

And again.

And again.

"Anyone? Is anyone there?"

He took a step back, frowning. Why would the gate have closed to him? Unless it was one of Gabriel's stupid jokes. Only, angels weren't exactly known for their sense of humor.

"Gabriel, is this your doing?"

It was not smart, pushing the archangel in front of everyone. Or, at least, if anyone bothered to listen. Was he even around? Had he learned Dante had gone against the grain and returned to Earth to investigate?

If he had, that still did not warrant barricading the gate for him. Perhaps it could have led to punishment, to some solitary confinement and forced meditation to think upon his sins, and cleanse his soul. It could have even ended with

Dante losing his privileges of coming and going of his own free will.

But to be refused entry? *It must be a misunderstanding. It has to be.*

He paced around, repeating his actions every once in a while. No matter what he did, no one came. Then the sun set, and the stars were out. Dante stared at them, recalling how they looked from the ground, how Earth had such a different take on it all.

Many a night, over the last twenty-five years, he'd glanced up at the stars and wished he was home. And then he'd finally gotten in, and the first thing he'd done was exit in order to follow some idiotic quest his good self could not let go of.

I failed. Or, in Daymun's words, he'd royally fucked up.

Just as his shoulders hunched, and he gave up hope of ever entering again, someone cleared their throat.

Dante turned to the gate and found none other than Gabriel waiting for him. The archangel's expression was unnaturally calm, almost bored.

"What is the meaning of this, Gabriel?" he asked, moving closer.

"Meaning? I know not what you speak of."

"Like hell! The gate will not open." To illustrate his point, he grabbed hold of the cool metal and jerked it a few times. He might as well have tried to move the Earth itself, for all the good it did.

Gabriel smirked, the first hint of an emotion. "Perhaps it has a reason."

"A reason?" Dante narrowed his eyes. "For me leaving? Are you saying the gate refuses me entrance because I took off of my own accord? What happened to freedom of will?"

"You are entitled to your freedom of will. Perhaps you did something else."

Dante tried to hold back his fury, but his body trembled with it. "Let me in."

"You know I cannot do so."

He meant it, too. Dante could see the resolution in his eyes, heard the determination in his voice. Or rather, the indifference. Gabriel would not lift a tiny finger to come to his aid.

For a moment, a brief second, he recalled Daymun's help. How his demon friend had dragged him across woods, monsters on their heels, until he'd found someone to help with his hurt wing. How he hadn't left him behind, and saved him from undue suffering. Would Gabriel have done the same?

In an effort to chase those thoughts away— and Daymun's angry expression, when he'd announced he was returning home—Dante cleared his throat. "I have news of Michael, the archangel."

Gabriel nodded. "Speak, then."

The fear in his gut grew heavier. Something was not right here, not at all. And whether it was Michael's own accusations that rang true in his ears, or his own assumptions, Dante was not about to dig himself into an even deeper hole.

"I will," he said. "In front of a witness."

Gabriel merely arched an eyebrow, then nodded. He lifted his hand and crooked his finger. A moment later, Ramona stepped out from behind him, her eyes filled with tears, her expression forlorn. Knowing he could no longer delay, Dante spoke.

"Michael is dead." Ramona's soft gasp made him pause to check for a reaction from

Gabriel, but his features were as immobile as marble. "He was attacked."

"And?"

The sensation in his gut increased. He was going to be sick, if he didn't get himself in check, and soon. "What do you mean, *and*? One of our own has died! Surely that justifies an investigation!"

"Was it his death that led you to Earth?"

"I... What?"

"Did you go there because you had magically learned of his death, or for other reasons?"

Dante looked away. "You know full well why I went."

"Then perhaps you should stop deluding yourself."

"What is that supposed to mean?"

"It means... Ramona, what is our commandment, as angels?"

"To not get involved."

Gabriel's expression lost its neutrality, but only Dante saw what shone through. Smugness. Victory.

"And what has our brother Dante been guilty of?"

"He... Getting involved." Her voice grew soft.

And there it was. Gabriel, archangel, using his own weakness against him. He should have been more careful. He should have taken precautions. Formed alliances. Not stumbled into this mess alone.

"You won't get away with this," Dante warned.

Gabriel laughed. "Get away with what, exactly? You are the one who broke the rules. You did not adhere to them when you had your protégée, and you definitely did not follow them now."

The words were out before he could stop them. "I had reason not to follow them with Katya!"

"Ah, do tell."

The amused glint in Gabriel's eyes should have cautioned him, but it did not. Dante said, "Something stank with Katya's entire trials, and you know it. One such thing was the fact we were to kill her! After accomplishing her tasks, Daymun and I were meant to *kill her*! An angel does not take a life. Is that not the rule? So how can you stand there, looking at me, and pretend everything is well?"

Gabriel shrugged. "I do not pretend anything. And I do not understand what you mean about killing the Flama. You have gotten too involved and are now speaking in delusions. It is what happens to our kind, and you will not regain entry while you are such."

Dante clenched his fists. "You cannot banish me from Heaven."

"I am not." Gabriel smiled. "I am letting you do penance."

"For something I did not do."

Gabriel scoffed again. "What you did and did not, is entirely between your conscience and the Creator. But as for what you are required to do... There is not much left of humanity, and your misgivings are the reason for it. The Flama may have chosen as she did, but she would not have embraced that particular path if you had done what I tasked you with. As you have broken our angel commandment, and become too involved, your punishment is to spend time on Earth, until such time as you are cleansed of your own delusions and can return here, pure and innocent, once more." Gabriel turned to leave. "Now if you will excuse me…"

Dante moved closer to the gate. "I will not let this stand."

Gabriel only laughed. And then, with a beat of his wings, the wind around them grew in force, until it tossed Dante through the Heavens, and back out of the portal. Away from home, and everything he cared for.

Chapter 10

Daymun

Daymun frowned at his surroundings. Twice now, he'd tried to call upon Hell and his connection, and it had been useless. He was still very much in the human woods, muttering about Dante abandoning him when they'd been so close, and unlikely to leave himself at this rate.

"What the bloody hell is going on?" he muttered.

First the demons had attacked them, then the archangel had died, and now the monastery.

Something was afoot, but how was he to fight such a battle, when it wasn't his? If anything, he should have been ensuring it took place as it was meant to, not stop it.

He grunted and tried once more to open Hell's gate, to the same effect. Then he moved over to a fallen tree trunk and perched himself on it. He pictured himself in a new, crispy business suit, and when he opened his eyes, his dirty pants, shoes, and torn shirt had been replaced by new ones. *At least when I finally enter Hell, I'll blend in.*

But his mind was no longer on his home. Instead, his thoughts kept going back to the paper he'd been given. The letter. The words written on it. The person who'd written them.

I am alive, and I am well... I only want my peace of mind. Let me have it, Daymun, please.

That sounded like Katya. And she was entitled to what she had earned.

Daymun knew, clear as the dawn almost breaking through, that he was done searching for her. After learning she had been meant to die by his hand, he was happy she had been spared. That he'd never had to make that choice, too. Eons ago, he would have, without a doubt. Now... *Never*.

Part of him was relieved, knowing she was alive. And another part... Knew it only meant more problems. He reached into his coat pocket, pulled the letter, and stared at it. Willed himself to burn it, to erase all traces of its existence. Before anyone else got their hands on it, before— worse—a demon like Asmodeus learned of her whereabouts.

The Dacians will look after her.

Though they might, it was best not to take any chances. Even as he pulled a breath and lifted his hand to light it, a voice echoed behind him.

"Did you get lost on the way home, lover?"

He tucked the paper back in his suit pocket, while he forced himself to turn around, as impassible as he could be. Demons were predictable, demonesses even more so. If he showed an inch of hesitation, of weakness, she would pounce.

What the hell is she even doing here?

"Fayana. Fancy meeting you here, love."

The words tasted like ash on his tongue, and he felt the weight of Katya's letter around his heart.

She sashayed towards him, eyes glittering in the darkness. "A good surprise, I take it?"

"One could say." He cleared his throat. "What happened with the gateway?"

"What do you mean?"

He narrowed his gaze on her, attempting to determine if she was toying with him. Surely, if she was on Earth, she had no issue using the gate. And if the restriction only applied to him... Perhaps he should avoid revealing his full hand, after all.

Daymun snorted. "Nothing. What brings you here?"

"I missed you," she purred and slithered closer to him. Her tongue snuck out and licked his jaw, even as her ever-wandering hands reached lower for the zipper of his pants.

His fingers tightened around her wrists. "What are you doing?"

Fayana bit her bottom lip. "What's it look like?" She pouted. "Once upon a time, you used to love this kind of play." The pout turned ugly.

"And then you had to spend a quarter of a century away. You've *changed*."

"You say it like it's a bad thing, love. I call it evolution."

She snorted under her breath, then moved closer. He angled his face to the side to avoid her kiss, but the movement had him lose sight of her hands for a split second. It was enough.

Fayana stepped backwards with a squeal of delight. "What is this, a secret letter?"

She waved it in the air. Though he tried to appear like it didn't matter, seeing Katya's letter in Fayana's grubby fingers drove him to the brink of destruction. He could feel his control snap, in a way it hadn't in eons.

Demons lived on drama. Fayana, more than most. If she caught a whiff of his anger—

Yet he could tell, just by her satisfied expression, that she already had. And he had no way to explain it, not really. He was no longer acting like a demon, at least not like one of his status was meant to act.

"*Please let me...*" Fayana mocked, and looked up at him, malice in her expression. "If I didn't know better, I'd say you *cared* for whoever this whore is."

"Watch your tone."

"Oooh, so you *do* care. Let me guess…" Her eyes widened, mocking him. "Is it the Flama? It's her, isn't it? *She's alive!* And you know where." She cackled. "I wonder what this information would be worth, in the hands of the right people."

She turned around to dance out of his grasp, but Daymun was faster. Older. More agile. And infinitely more determined. One moment Fayana was sprinting about, the next he'd moved quicker than even vampires could. He'd only meant to grip her throat, warn her to shut up.

And yet, barely seconds later, he found himself with Fayana's head in his hand, her neck severed clean. Dark blood spouted out of the wound, and her beheaded body fell with a thud.

"Well, fuck." Daymun let the head drop, and it rolled away from him, bouncing on the soft grass and leaving burgundy trails behind. "Now every demon in the vicinity's going to pop by and have a sniff. Nothing like a fallen comrade to attract them."

Daymun pursed his lips in disgust. He

204 ♆ ALEXA WHITEWOLF

hadn't meant to kill her, not really. But in his desire to get rid of the letter, to remove all traces of what she had learned, he had gotten overeager, as used to be his way.

Remorse was not part of his personality, yet even he knew he could have handled the matter better. After wiping his hands on his pants, he bent and picked up Katya's last message, now tainted with blood.

"You couldn't leave it well enough alone, could you?" he asked Fayana's corpse.

There would be no fixing this dead demon, that much was for sure. With a groan, he stood and stepped backwards. One swipe of his hand, and flames burst through the grass, burning Fayana's body to ashes. He watched until there was nothing left of her, then glanced at the letter one more time.

It was too dangerous to be held in his hands. Way too risky to hide anywhere, after all. "Sentimentality doesn't suit you," he mumbled to himself.

With a sigh, he let the message fall into the flames, watching as it was destroyed within seconds.

"Enjoy your peace, Katya." He lifted his eyes to skies. "As much as possible, I'll try to keep this war away from your door. I may not win, but I'll do my damnedest."

He turned his back on the fire, only to be met with large, thick shadows. And out of them stepped none other than Asmodeus.

Chapter 11

Daymun

"Asmodeus."

Daymun tried to remain cool, but he knew he'd been caught red-handed. Killing a demon was not a crime, in the least. But the reasons behind it... Rage could be understood. Protection for another being, especially a human? Not likely.

How long has he been here? That's the real question. And how can I figure it out without giving away what I've done?

He willed his features to remain neutral and dug his hands in his pockets to appear as nonchalant as possible. "What wind of fate led you here?"

"Same as everyone else." Asmodeus stepped closer, looked around, sniffed the air. "Trying to see what our kin finds so... fascinating... about this decrepit world. My soldiers tell me it is quite tasty."

Daymun didn't rise to the bait. Instead, he kept his breathing calm and gave a stiff smile. "Perhaps the never-ending supply of prey."

"Ah, yes. I have heard Beelzebub's men have much fun with the human females."

Stay cool. He's provoking you on purpose. Out loud, he forced what he hoped was a neutral enough answer. "Interesting."

Daymun didn't even care about humans. So why the sudden blazing fire in the pit of his stomach, and the need to wipe the smirk off Asmodeus' face? Was Fayana correct, and he truly had changed so much in only twenty-five years?

Impossible.

"I take it old Fayana stopped serving her purpose, then?"

Daymun glanced behind himself and shrugged. "She questioned my authority. It was time to put her in her place."

"Hmm." Asmodeus moved closer still, circling until some of the dying flames were between them. "Funny. From where I was standing, it seemed she had learned something you didn't want her to."

Stay. Cool.

"Such as?"

"The truth behind certain rumors about a certain shifter we both know. One I had hoped you could find for me."

Daymun dropped the act. The fire in his gut eased, replaced instead by a calmness he was unaccustomed to. He should have felt fear, or wariness given the danger he was in. His mind had already made the connections between Asmodeus and Fayana being there at the same time—he had gotten played. And, unfortunately, revealed his hand.

The best that could happen would be Asmodeus punishing him again, but allowing his return to Hell. The worst? That was another story altogether. The only question left was how far he'd go to protect Katya's secret—and what remained of the world. Especially when the only person who should have cared had returned to the Silver fucking City.

"I take it, then, that you're the reason behind my being unable to return to Hell?" Daymun asked.

Asmodeus laughed. "Perhaps you have simply—what do humans say—forgotten your key."

"Don't fucking play me, you wanker. We both know this is rubbish. I delivered the end of the world on a platter. The only reason you hate it, it's because it was delivered by *me*." Daymun snorted. "And not by your lazy arse."

Asmodeus' entire features changed with anger. "How dare you speak to a Prince of Hell like this?"

Daymun rolled his eyes. "Not this again. Fucking give me my punishment or leave already. Or better yet, open the gate so I can return home."

A smile of satisfaction spread on Asmodeus' features. "Haven't you figured it out yet?"

"Figured out what?"

"There is no return home for you. You will not be back in Hell, not for a while."

Daymun tapped his leg with his left hand, to distract his mind from his flaring temper. "This is outrageous. I demand to speak to Lucifer."

"The Prince of Darkness has better things to do than listen to your whining."

"I bet that's not true."

Asmodeus looked up from his nails, a sly smile on his lips. "Yet you have no way of proving it."

"What do you want?" Daymun growled.

He had to hand it to him. The higher demon was good at building suspense. Asmodeus walked the entire length of the meadow once, twice, peering at the spot Fayana's body had burned on and clicking his tongue.

"Give me the Flama," he said while staring at the ground, "and I will allow you entrance to Hell."

"No."

Asmodeus looked up into Daymun's lethal expression. "Not even thinking about it?"

"There's nothing to think about."

He had not pursued Katya's existence for so long, and gone through the hoops of the last days, for no reason. And especially not to betray her.

Asmodeus laughed. "How misplaced your loyalty is, demon. No matter. As I said, you are to remain here, away from Hell, and pay your penance."

Daymun opened his mouth to speak but before he could, Asmodeus lifted his hands. Chains of fire rose from the ground and wrapped around his ankles and wrists, until they tugged him to his knees. Then they tightened around his joints, and he heard the sizzle of his clothes.

Still, he would not scream. He gritted his teeth and looked up into Asmodeus' face. And what he saw there...was pure, cold satisfaction. Enough to finally click the last of the puzzle pieces into place.

"You killed the archangel, didn't you?" Daymun asked.

"I know not what you speak of."

Daymun laughed. "Oh, but you do. And I bet you sent the rogue demons after me and the angel, too."

Asmodeus said nothing.

"The only question is, why? What do you get out of it, unless you're playing the game... And playing you are, I bet." He glanced at his wrists. "Let me go, Asmodeus, and I won't tell on you. It'll be our little secret."

"No." Asmodeus moved closer. "I believe I am done pretending to be a just ruler and merciful lord. You and I have had our last face-to-face, demon." His fingers turned into claws, and they swiped at Daymun's face.

The blow struck with all the force of a freight train, shredding the skin and muscle underneath. This time, Daymun did scream, unable to hold back the raw cry of pain escaping him. The well-aimed hit had not only torn off half his cheek but also sent poison into his skin, into his being—and it weakened him.

Asmodeus lifted his other hand, ready to deliver the same blow—but a sword came out of nowhere and stopped him.

Even more, it slashed cleanly around his wrist, effectively ridding him of his hand. Asmodeus stumbled backwards, staring as black blood gushed out of the stump of his elbow. He raised wide eyes to the winged man landing in front of Daymun. The one with an angel's blade.

"Dante, don't—"

Too late. The celestial had already lifted the sword, and with one clean swipe, he snuffed out Asmodeus' existence. Then he undid Daymun's bindings, the metal of the sword cutting through the fire and snuffing it out.

Rather than be overjoyed, he stumbled to his feet, watching the demon disintegrate into nothingness. He raised a shocked gaze to Dante. "What've you done?"

"Saved your life, for once. You are welcome, demon."

Chapter 12

Dante

Despite a chance to be thankful, all Daymun did was stare in shock. Finally, he shook his head. "This is bad. Asmodeus was a Prince of Hell. One of the six serving under Lucifer."

Dante heard him, and the words did register. But he was too busy staring at the dark blood on his blade, and the demon's body burning up in ashes. What had he done?

"And?" he asked, his voice sounding faraway.

"And? Are you bloody blind? You've just turned him into ashy cabbage rolls! This means we'll be hunted, both of us. It'll be easy for you, Heaven will protect you, but given what Michael said—And what are you even doing back here? Weren't you on your way home?"

Dante finally snapped out of his daze and glanced around. "Yes, I was." There was no return, not now. He had fought and killed to save Daymun, but no one in the Silver City would understand him breaking the commandment to defend a demon. Had this been another trap of Gabriel's? Did it even matter?

"Had second thoughts, then?" Daymun asked, frowning.

"Not quite." Dante decided honesty was his best bet. "More like I was not allowed to enter."

Daymun stopped pacing and rubbed his pained wrists, then his cheek. "Huh?"

"I arrived at the gate of Heaven. And it would not open for me."

"Funny. Hell wouldn't for me, either."

Dante felt as if he'd been punched. "Then we are both doomed. To be on Earth, away from our true homes, with no protection. For-ever living with the choices we made." Some more life-destroying than others.

"Perhaps doomed isn't the way to look at it."

Daymun sighed. With a sweep of his hand, he called forth more flames to incinerate the rest of Asmodeus. When the monster was fully gone, he turned to Dante.

"We need to leave here. Anywhere else, somewhere far away, where the demons haven't yet gotten. Find us a spot, will you?"

Dante nodded. "I know of one." He stepped closer and held out his hand, knowing Daymun would be able to see what he did.

When the demon finally touched him, Dante closed his eyes and pictured the area. The hill slope, the remnants of a castle, towers reaching strong and time-defying. A bridge led inside to a massive courtyard, surrounded by walls of gold, yellow and dark brick.

A place of safety. A place of... organization. One he had discovered long ago, in one of Katya's books, and had visited by himself at the first opportunity.

He opened his eyes, trying to suppress the peace he'd felt when seeing it.

"What was that?" Daymun asked. He, too, seemed shaken.

"Humans called it Stirling Castle. It is abandoned now, given the state of things, and would serve as a convenient fortress. A good spot to hide until our next move."

Daymun nodded, needing no further convincing. "See you there, then."

It took Dante only hours to get from Romania's hills and valleys to the castle. If nothing else, his almost-inside-the-Silver-City trip had healed his wing, enough so he could fly again. He doubted the pain would ever truly disappear, but at least it was usable.

Though the journey was short, it was also eye-opening. Too much so. Everywhere his eyes fell, he saw destruction. Larger cities were wiped completely. Smoke and ashes rose from them, buildings were tumbled and abandoned, not a soul to be seen. Dante had gotten closer to ground around some of the capitals—Munich, Paris, London—and it was the same everywhere. He recalled what Ramona had said about the demons not trying to hide in the overly populated areas.

And when he poked in the shadows, he could hear their scuttling paws—demons—as they waited for darkness. Entire cities infested, but with pests much more dangerous than the original humans.

In the countryside, the damage was even more visible. Large patches of forests were completely razed to the ground. Bodies were piled in town squares like trophies. Were the demons making a game of this?

Disgusted, Dante turned away and tried to keep his stomach from roiling over. Ramona had been right, and he should have listened. What his eyes witnessed... *I must stop it. Protect them. Somehow.*

As he'd promised, the castle was empty and abandoned. He landed on the upper tower, and lower still, could see Daymun in what used to be a garden. Now, it was burned to the ground, with litter everywhere. Human, or demonic damage?

Dante sent forth a wind to clean it, which automatically also announced his presence to his friend.

Friend... Is that really what he is to me, then? He'd gone back and forth over designations, but there was no other way to put it. After all, he had committed the ultimate treason as far as Heaven was concerned—murder. And it had been to save a demon.

Dante shook his head and allowed his wings to flap. He landed near Daymun this time. "What do you think?"

Daymun whistled, eyes roaming everywhere. They had a perfect view of anyone attacking, while being behind thickly reinforced walls. A safe spot.

"It'll do," he finally said.

"You seemed deep in thought."

"Probably because we don't have a lot of time."

Daymun turned to him. His cheek was still scarred, massively so. Dante thought he could see a hint of bone under all the red, torn flesh. In time, it would heal—not that its presence seemed to affect the demon's energy. On the contrary, he was practically bouncing on the balls of his feet.

"Alright, here's the deal, mate. You missed a bit with the Dacian earlier."

"Which bit?"

"The part where he gave me a letter from Katya, saying she's well and truly alive and where I was warned she won't join this new coming battle. The Dacians will protect her, that much was laid bare for me to understand."

"We cannot fault her for that, given what we were told about our true purpose." Dante rubbed his chin. "I am... happy for her."

"As am I."

"So you found your answers, then?"

"In a way."

Dante nodded. "Did you tell Mihai about the Ossi, and Michael's death?"

"He already knew, believe it or not. He filled me in on a few things, though."

Dante listened intently as Daymun related the Dacian's words. He tried not to appear surprised that a human had knowledge of such things, but it was hard. Plainly, the surprise was on his features, as Daymun picked up on it.

"Yeah, I know. He shocked me, too."

"I suppose it will be one mystery left for later, then." Dante moved his wings, his gaze turning to the horizon. Soon, it would be night.

"It still leaves questions," Daymun said. "Like why was our path home blocked? Why've we been thrust into this new mess? And how're we supposed to fix it? That's my problem."

"I dare say they do not expect us to." Dante mulled over his words. "Gabriel was adamant I had done wrong, that I did not deserve to return to the Silver City. Yet, it is clear he was involved with Michael's death. He was not surprised."

"And I'd wager Asmodeus was, as well."

Dante frowned. A shudder ran through him. "Surely... A Prince of Hell, and an archangel, an Elder, of Heaven?"

"Don't you recall what Michael said? The battle *is* between our two worlds. And whether or not we like it, one key piece to winning it are the humans."

"The same humans Katya unleashed Hell upon."

"Mm."

They both moved closer to the edge of the fortress, glancing beneath. Everywhere, their gazes landed on ruins of what had once been Stirling. Houses demolished. Churches burned. And far in the distance, unharmed, the Wallace Monument overlooked the leftovers of this part of the human world. Even farther, a few fires flickered, like signals of hope.

"Humanity has been thrust back into the medieval times," Dante whispered.

"Try the Dark Ages," Daymun added. "And good luck to them surviving it all again."

Silence lengthened between them, but with each passing second it became heavier and heavier with meaning. Dante felt a rush of something go through him—it took him a moment to recognize excitement.

"That is the answer!"

"What?"

"We are forced to stay here, and we know the battle will involve the humans. So, we build our army."

Daymun let out a low whistle. "It's official. You're delusional."

"Hear me out before you dismiss me easily. We both have the skills."

"And who would we choose for this magical army? Mortals, who can readily die? Dacians, who care only for themselves?"

The more Dante thought about it, the crazier the idea became. But he had crossed every line there was and could no longer discount it. The truth was there, plain as day. They only had to be brave enough to seize it.

"No…" He grinned, albeit manically. "We will get half-demons."

"*What?*"

For once, he had succeeded in shocking Daymun. He would have taken a moment to celebrate, were it not too imperative he get his point across, and fast.

"Your demons, on this Earth, are prone to having progeny. We will seek out those who present specific gifts, and I will use my celestial blood to bind them."

"Bind them how? Is that even possible?"

"Yes, it is. It has been done before— Michael showed me how, when he mentored me. And it is used to temper down their demonic influence and ensure they will apply their demonic powers for good."

Daymun shook his head. "And what'll this achieve, exactly? Besides headaches, and quite a lot of half-demons for us to babysit?"

"It will provide us with an army, something we can use to protect humanity, and fight against whatever will come."

"Or, we could sit back and do nothing."

Dante watched him closely. "Can you really live with that option? For all eternity?"

Daymun was silent for a while. Too long. In the end, he ran a hand over his face. "No. I'm not, and you bloody well know it. For whatever idiotic, rubbish reason, your idea is the best we have. So, how do we get started?"

"You are the Hell connection. Know of any candidates we can keep an eye on?"

Silence again. Then, slowly, Daymun grinned. "Not yet, but I'm sure we can find someone."

Epilogue

25 years later...

"Daymun, wait!"

"If you'd hurry, I wouldn't have to!"

They were in the middle of a forest. Again. Dante should have been used to it by now. Heaven knew they'd sought many half-demons in their quest to build their army. And it hadn't gone well. Not always.

"We have been seeking them for a quarter of a century. Surely she can wait a little longer."

Daymun snorted up ahead. "Are you saying

you want to keep saving humans, just the two of us? That game got boring twenty-four years ago, mate."

A sigh escaped Dante. He could have flown, rather than continue the treacherous hike uphill. But over the years, he'd forced himself to rely less and less on his wings—especially given the more he'd stayed on Earth, the longer his hurt one pained him.

"All I ask is that you wait!" he shouted.

"Nope." Without looking back, Daymun continued onwards, as if to spite him.

No. There was no *as if* to it. The demon *was* doing it to spite him, knowing full well Dante much preferred a cautious approach to barging in recklessly. They might have worked side by side for a half-century thus far—slowly trying to piece together their army, while saving humans whenever an opportunity presented itself—but it didn't mean they got along any better.

"Daymun, we could have started with the boy. He is—"

"Yeah, yeah, your champion. I've heard it all before. Well, she's my pick, so suck it up, celestial."

Dante finally caught up with his counterpart and gripped his arm. But it was already too late. They had made their way uphill, to the little fire they'd spotted while on their journey back home to Sterling. Daymun had sworn far and wide that he sensed another potential—*his* own pick of a champion—and before Dante could manage to talk him out of it, they were heading towards her.

"Shit," Dante muttered.

As always when Daymun took the lead, they'd walked straight into a... situation.

Around the fire they'd spotted was a group of demons—rather, half-demons. Their human features easily gave them away. And they did not seem happy at the interruption, even less so when they noticed Dante's ivory wings.

Daymun said nothing, only yanked out of his grasp and turned to them. At the same time, a girl stood in the grouping's midst. She had hair the color of a raven's, cat-like eyes rimmed with red, and was dressed in dark clothing. Tight, dark clothing, which if Dante was not mistaken, was tainted with blood. Unless his nose betrayed him.

In her left hand, she held a curved, meat-cleaver type of knife, sizeable enough to do some real damage. His gaze stayed glued to it for a lengthier moment, given the last time he'd been around blades, it had not ended well. Then he continued his observations, down to her boot-clad feet and discarded bow and arrows—clearly, she preferred to do her killing up close.

"Who the fuck are you losers?" she asked.

Daymun chuckled. Dante wished he could find amusement in the situation, but judging by the other half-demons and their increasingly darkening auras, they didn't have much time.

"Daymun—" Though his voice was low, demonic ears twitched in the distance. They'd heard him.

"Daymun?" One demon called out. "Like the one kicked out of Hell?"

The girl's eyes narrowed on them, then a slow smile graced her lips. It looked deadly.

"That's why your face was familiar." As if mesmerized, she inched closer.

She couldn't have been over five feet tall, but the way she carried herself said she was not afraid of them. The blackness of her stare shone in direct contrast with the rim of burgundy around the irises. When she smiled, her canines showed a little too sharp, like they'd been purposefully filed. And the closer she moved, the more Dante realized he'd been right—it was definitely blood he smelled on her clothes.

She came to an abrupt stop a few feet away from them. Then she smirked. "Too slow."

A moment after, she shot the knife towards Daymun. He caught it between his fingers and returned the smirk, taking a step closer despite Dante's hissed warning. "Amara, love, let's have a chat, shall we?"

Despite the years, he still hadn't dropped the English accent, nor had he learned to properly use his gender-focused terms. Not that Amara seemed impressed. If anything, she frowned, taken aback by the fact he knew her name.

"About what?" she asked.

Something about her stance warned Dante things were not all they were meant to be. And, judging by Amara's companions, they were about to have yet another fight on their hands.

Daymun, however, had no such qualms. Dressed in his signature fancy suit, he simply strode forward, assured and too darned confident of his win. "We'd like a chat about a brotherhood we want you to join... The Demoni Sancti."

When he moved out of the way, Dante saw the glint of a knife in Amara's hand. Good thing he'd guessed as much and had already whipped out his trusty celestial sword. With one push of his legs, he was lunging in the air to cover his partner's back.

As he flew over Daymun, he tossed down, "Told you we should have gone with the guy first."

To be continued....

In the next installment, the Demoni Sancti brotherhood takes on their purpose – salvation of the remaining humanity. Find out how Amara and Dante's champion, Rowan, get along—or, don't.

Can half-demons truly work together and fight their basic impulses? Or will the

brotherhood fall apart before it even has a
chance?
And what of Daria, the Ossi, and the
angel-demon conspiracy?
Find that out & more in...
BROKEN (Demoni Sancti #2)

Pre-order it today!

*And if you enjoyed Dante & Daymun,
please consider leaving a review at your
choice of retailer. Even a line or two makes a
huge difference as an indie author!*

ACKNOWLEDGEMENTS

This new series wouldn't have come to life without the copious amounts of coffee ingested somewhere in the summer of 2020 as I decided to try writing 2 books in one month! Fun times... 😊

As always, thanks where it's due, to all the amazing people that have helped me on this journey!

To Steven, for being the best husband I can ask for!

To my mom, for loving me unconditionally!

To my furry babies, for reminding me to take a breather and unplugging my laptop when I get a migraine so I can get some sleep!

To Siobhan and Kristina for the awesome feedback that helped make this book truly shine!

To the awesome team at LIAS for the editing and masterful formatting, you guys rock!

To my cover designer, Y. Nikolova at Ammonia Book Covers, for a truly awesome cover!!

ABOUT THE AUTHOR

Alexa Whitewolf is a fiction writer, newspaper columnist of daily issues and author of the critically acclaimed *Moonlight Rogues* shifter series.

Alexa has been a lifelong writer and first began creating other worlds and characters at the ripe age of 12. Growing up in the Transylvania region surrounded by epic mountains and a never-ending stream of legends and stories was bound to create an overactive imagination. This shines through Ms. Whitewolf's writing by creating worlds filled with unique folklore, life wisdom and plenty of furry creatures.

An avid traveler, Alexa writes under a penname and spends her days between an office job and writing in Canada's capital, when she's not flying somewhere with lush landscapes and plenty of hiking trails.

Her series focus on strong heroines, kind yet sexy men, fights of good and evil and the never-ending learning curve of humanity's strong— and weak—points. Romanian folklore is intertwined with her writing, more notably in her shifter romance series, the *Moonlight Rogues*. Her other series draw on world mythology, such as the Avalon myth and Arthurian legend (*The Avalon Chronicles*) and Ancient Egypt (*The Sage's Legacy*).

You can follow her blog at www.alexawhitewolf.com/blog or on social media. Her column in Observatorul also tackles various issues, including health, technology, and a writer's life.

If you want up to date releases, make sure you sign up for her newsletter. For new releases notifications, you can also follow her on Amazon or BookBub.

Also by the Author

Demoni Sancti Extended Universe

Standalone
Blazing Ashes

Demoni Sancti series
Fallen
Broken
Unshackled
Risen
Ascended

Rogues Extended Universe

Moonlight Rogues series
Moonlight Rogues: Origins
First to Fall
Second to Surrender
Third to Tumble
Last to Love

Flaming Rogues series
Fanning the Flames

Igniting the Ice

Immortal Rogues series
Shadowy Secrets
Archer's Arrow
Cat's Charms
Trickster's Trap
Fickle Fate

Lost Royals of Transylvania series
Immortal Illusion
Cracked Casualty
Deadly Deceit
Blind Burden
Angry Addiction
Primal Protection

The Avalon Chronicles series
Avalon Dreams
Avalon Wishes
Avalon Nightmares
Atrox

The Sage's Legacy – YA series
The Dragon Medallion

The Dragon Manuscript
Relics of the Underworld

Standalone novels
Blood Ties, Love Binds
Unconditional Love